rhcbooks.com

ISBN 978-0-7364-3997-8 (hardcover)
ISBN 978-0-7364-3998-5 (paperback)

Printed in the United States of America
10 9 8 7 6 5 4 3 2 1

The Deluxe Junior Novelization

Adapted by Suzanne Francis

Random House 🏠 New York

Prologue

Once, about ten years ago, in a boy named Andy's room . . .

Lightning flashed through the window and thunder rumbled. Jessie, a cowgirl toy, and her horse, Bullseye, looked out into the dark night as the storm raged.

"Whoa!" exclaimed Jessie. "It's raining cats and dogs out there! I hope they make it back all right. . . ."

The sound of quick footsteps coming toward the bedroom made the toys gasp.

"Heads up!" said a pink piggy bank named Hamm. "Andy's coming!"

The toys collapsed into toy mode as Andy, energetic and eight years old, burst into the room, soaking wet and smiling. He dropped an armful of wet toys onto his bed and ran down to dinner.

As soon as Andy left, Sheriff Woody snapped out of toy mode, jumped down from the bed, and darted to the windowsill. He began scanning the yard.

"Do you see him?" asked Buzz Lightyear, a space ranger action figure, as he climbed up to the sill.

"No," said Woody.

"Well, he's done for," said Slinky Dog, his tail and coils drooping.

"He'll be lost!" said Rex the dinosaur, his voice quaking with anxiety. "Forever!"

Woody jumped to the floor and began giving orders. "Jessie. Buzz. Slink. Molly's room. The rest of you, stay put."

Woody headed to the open door and down the hall. He peeked into Molly's bedroom and smiled when he saw Bo, a Little Bo Peep porcelain doll figurine, who stood on her lamp base next to her sheep. Bo belonged to Andy's little sister, Molly, but she was close friends with Woody and the rest of the toys in Andy's room. The cutouts in Bo's lamp's rotating shade created gentle points of light, like twinkling stars, all over the room.

Woody climbed up the nightstand toward Bo. She knew something was up and held out her staff to help him. "Situation?" she asked.

"Lost toy," said Woody. "Side yard."

"Billy. Goat. Gruff," commanded Bo. "Raise the blinds."

Without a second thought, the three sheep bit down on the cord to the blinds and leaped off the nightstand, raising the blinds as they dropped to the floor.

Woody, Bo, Jessie, and Buzz gaped out the window as the rain slapped against it, making it difficult to see. Finally, they spotted him. RC, a remote-control car, was stuck in the muddy water rushing toward the storm drain at the end of the driveway. He spun his wheels as he tried to get out, but he only sank deeper and deeper.

Bo and Woody looked at each other for a brief moment as they plotted their next move. The friends had a way of communicating without words.

They both turned to the room and announced, "Operation Pull Toy!"

Working together, the toys launched Jessie into the air to unlock the window. Then Bo wedged her staff under the bottom of the window, forcing it open.

Woody and Bo leaned over the ledge, gazing down at the stranded car. Bo turned to Woody and straightened his hat. The cowboy took a deep breath, smiled, and hopped on top of Slinky. Buzz and Jessie held Slinky's back end while Woody took a running leap out the window with the toy's front end.

In the pouring rain, Woody rappelled down the side of the house to the ground. He spotted RC struggling in the storm drain.

The little vehicle spun his wheels in the mud, trying to get closer to Woody, but the rushing water kept pulling him away. The cowboy stretched Slinky as far as he could go, but they weren't able to reach the car.

"I ain't got any more slink!" cried Slinky.

Bo watched from the window as Woody held one of Slinky's paws, stretching a bit farther, but it still wasn't enough. Woody hooked the plastic loop of his pull string over Slinky's paw, and that wasn't enough, either.

He looked back to see Bo at the window, holding her staff with an entire barrel's worth of monkeys linked together. She had added them to Slinky's line, giving Woody the boost he needed. With a big lunge forward, he grabbed RC!

Woody gave the others the signal to pull, but just as he and RC sprang up, a car drove into Andy's driveway. The toys were quick, but not quick enough. Buzz and the gang hauled the exhausted toy car into the bedroom, and—*WHAP!* The window slammed down on Slinky before he and Woody could make it inside.

Woody scrambled up to the ledge and peeked through the window. In the bedroom, Molly and Andy's mom was talking with the man from the car.

"I'm so glad to see this old lamp go to a good home," she said to him.

He watched in horror as Molly and Andy's mom placed Bo, her lamp, and her sheep into a cardboard box and handed it to the man. After thanking her, he turned and asked, "Molly, are you sure it's all right?"

"Yeah, I don't want it anymore," Molly said without hesitation.

The people walked out, and the toys rushed to the window, working together to pull the rest of Slinky up.

"Where's Woody?" asked Buzz, surprised to see his friend wasn't there.

Out in the driveway, the man put the cardboard box down behind his car as he searched his pockets for his keys. Unable to find them, he groaned and jogged back to the house.

As soon as he left, the box was pulled underneath the car. Its flaps were opened, and when a bolt of lightning flashed, Woody peered into the box and saw Bo comforting her sheep.

"Quick!" Woody said. "We'll sneak into the hedges before he's back—"

"Woody, it's okay . . . ," said Bo, her voice calm and steady.

"Wha—? No! No, no. You can't go. What's best for Andy is that you—"

"Woody. I'm not Andy's toy," said Bo. Woody stared for a moment, but he knew she was right.

"It's time for the next kid," Bo continued. They heard the front door open and knew they didn't have much time. "You know, kids lose their toys every day. Sometimes they get left in the yard . . . or put in the wrong box." She smiled as she waited for Woody's reply. She was hoping he would join her.

"And that box gets taken away . . . ," said Woody, considering her idea, grasping the edges of the cardboard box.

But the sound of Andy's voice stopped him in his tracks.

"Mom, where's Woody?" he asked, concerned. Woody and Bo saw Andy run out the front door. "I can't find Woody!"

Woody sagged and let go of the box. He could never leave Andy, knowing how much his kid needed him. Bo was sad, but she understood why Woody had to stay. She reached out and straightened his hat one last time. After wiping a raindrop from his cheek, she smiled and settled back in beside her sheep.

Seconds later, the man returned and the car backed out of the driveway, revealing Woody on the ground, in toy mode. Woody stared at the car's lights, watching them shrink until they disappeared into the stormy night.

Andy sighed with relief when he saw Woody in the rainy driveway. "There you are!" he said, scooping him up. "Mom, I found him!" Andy's mom chuckled as she ushered him inside and closed the door.

Andy's toys loved life with Andy. He was a joyful, imaginative kid who played with them all the time. Andy's favorite was Woody, and that made him the leader of the toys. Andy took Woody just about everywhere he went.

But the years went by, and when Andy grew up, he wanted to pass his toys on to someone new. Bonnie, a playful little girl down the street, was a lot like Andy when he was a kid. He knew she would be the perfect person to take care of his toys. When Andy gave Woody to Bonnie, she hugged the toy close.

"My cowboy!" she said. Then she flew him around the yard, just like Andy used to. She tugged on his pull string and laughed as his voice box said, "You're my favorite deputy!"

Andy was right—Bonnie was a wonderful kid for a toy. She wrote her name on the bottom of Woody's boot, and Woody knew he and the rest of Andy's toys were in good hands. But as time went on, Woody found himself being played with less and less. Soon he was watching playtime from the sidelines.

Bonnie's toys were crammed inside her bedroom closet, waiting to play.

"It's getting hot in here," said Trixie, a toy dinosaur.

"Where's my ear?" said Mr. Potato Head.

"Ow! Hey, quit shoving!" said Buttercup, a stuffed unicorn.

"Sorry," said Trixie. "That was my horn."

Dolly, the leader of Bonnie's toys, stood on a stack of board games. "Everyone listen. I thought I told you—when Mom quickly cleans the bedroom like that, expect to be put in the closet."

Woody wandered through the toys, checking on his friends to make sure they were all okay.

Jessie, uncomfortable in the dark closet, was breathing fast.

"Deep breaths, Jessie," said Woody, trying to calm her. "Deep breaths." He walked by Slinky, whose wagging tail was jangling his metal coils. "Settle down, Slink. Sit. Good boy."

Dolly stepped up to Woody. "Sheriff, do I need to be worried?"

"Nah, nah, nah," said Woody. "My guys are veterans. They'll hang in there."

"Good. Just keep 'em calm until we get word," said Dolly.

Woody saluted her. "Yes, ma'am." He headed off and began pacing back and forth.

Buzz watched Woody, concerned. "How are you, uh . . . feeling about today?" he asked.

"Uh, good, good," said Woody. "Yeah . . . good. I'm good."

Buzz frowned, trying to read Woody's expression. He could see his friend was nervous about playtime but didn't want to talk about it. "Uh . . . good," said Buzz.

Dolly's attention turned to the slats in the closet door as she peered at a toy dangling from the bedroom doorknob. The toy kicked its legs, causing bells to chime, a warning that Bonnie was coming.

Dolly faced everyone and reported the news. "We're on. Bonnie's done with breakfast."

"Any minute now," said Dolly.

"Ya hear that?" said Woody, turning to his crew. "Any minute now. Wind 'em if you got 'em. Keep your batteries clean. Your joints unlocked."

"Thanks, Woody. I got it," said Dolly, trying to remind him that she was in charge.

"Yes, I'm sorry," said Woody. He had led Andy's toys for so long that he often forgot it wasn't his job anymore.

The toys went silent when they heard the sound of small, quick footsteps in the hall. Before they knew it, the closet door was flung open and Bonnie shouted, "The town is open!" She scooped up her toys and placed them all around, creating a pretend town.

"Hi, mayor!" she said, grabbing Dolly. "Banker!" She grabbed Hamm. "Hi, ice cream man!" She picked up Slinky. "Hat-shop owner," she said when she held Trixie. "Mailman." She grabbed Buzz.

"And the sheriff!" Bonnie picked up Woody, but she didn't take him out of the closet to play. She plucked the badge from his shirt and dropped him back to the floor.

"Okay—bye, toys!" Bonnie closed the door and began to play on the carpet.

Woody looked through the slats in the door and watched Bonnie put Woody's badge on Jessie's shirt and hold her up.

"YEE-HAW! Sheriff Jessie!" she said. "Giddyup, Bullseye!"

Woody sat up and noticed that he wasn't alone in the closet. There were some toddler toys nearby, looking at him with pity. Woody ignored their sad faces and pulled out a deck of cards to play by himself. The toddler toys shuffled closer to the closet door to watch through the slats as Bonnie and the others played hat shop.

An old toy clock gazed at Woody. "That's the third time you haven't been picked this week," he said. Woody continued to focus on the cards.

"I don't know. I don't keep count," said Woody, slightly irritated.

"Oh, you don't have to. I'll do it for you!" said the clock.

"Okay, okay, okay. I get it. It's been a while," said Woody, his voice sounding strained. He walked away and peered through the door slats with the toddler toys.

"Bonnie?" her dad said as he entered the bedroom. "Go get your shoes on, we gotta go. You don't want to be late for kindergarten orientation, do you?"

Bonnie's smile fell as she looked at the floor. "But . . . I don't want to go," she said quietly.

"We talked about this," said her dad. "We're going to meet your teachers, see your classroom—" He tried to sound upbeat.

"Can I bring a toy?" she asked.

"Toys don't go to school, that's the rule," he said. He took her hand and gently led her out of the room.

Dolly popped up. "Freeze!" she shouted. "Nobody move! Bonnie always forgets something. She'll be back any second."

Woody opened the closet door and quickly walked past Buzz.

"You all right, Woody? I'm sure she'll pick you next time," said Buzz.

"Come on," Woody said with a chuckle, "I'm fine, no problem."

Jessie scurried over. "Hey, Woody. Here," she said, handing him his badge. The cowboy thanked her and continued to walk toward Dolly as he pinned the badge back onto his shirt. Buzz and Jessie exchanged a concerned look.

"Scuse me, Dolly?" said Woody.

"Woody, can't you see I'm threatening everyone? Go back to the closet!" she ordered.

"Yeah, I know, I know," said Woody. "It's just—I'm worried about Bonnie. A toy should go with her to orientation."

Dolly ushered him back toward the closet. "Didn't you hear Dad?" she said sternly. "You'll get Bonnie in trouble."

"Yeah, but kindergarten is so different. It can be too much for a kid. Having a buddy with them to get through it can really help things. I remember with Andy, I would go to school with him—"

"Uh-huh. I'm sorry, Woody," said Dolly,

annoyed. "I hate to sound like a broken record, but Bonnie is not Andy."

"No, no, no, of course, I get that, but if you would just hear me—"

Before he could finish, Dolly shut the closet door with Woody inside. "Places, everyone!" she whispered loudly.

Bonnie burst back into her bedroom and threw herself under the bed, crying.

Her mom came into the room, followed closely by her dad. They gently coaxed Bonnie out until she wiped her eyes, took a deep breath, and got up. "That's my big girl."

"Don't forget your backpack," added her dad.

Bonnie grabbed it from the floor.

"You're gonna have so much fun . . . ," her mom said as they all left together.

Dolly opened the closet door and peered inside. "All right. Now, what was it you were saying, Woody?"

The preschool toys looked at her blankly.

"Woody?" Dolly looked around for him, confused. Woody wasn't there.

2

Bonnie slumped in the backseat of the car. Woody, peering through a small open space at the zipper of her backpack, looked up at her, concerned.

Soon they reached the school. Bonnie clung to her mom's hand as they walked up the steps, then went inside and down the hall to the kindergarten classroom. She glanced around at all the other kids in the class before burying her face in her mom's leg.

"Bonnie, honey, it'll be okay," her mom said.

The teacher noticed Bonnie right away and knelt in front of her with a bright smile.

"Hi," she said. "Are you Bonnie?"

Bonnie peeked out from behind her mom's leg but didn't say a word.

"My name is Miss Wendy," the teacher continued. "I'm going to be your kindergarten teacher. We have a special place where you can put your backpack. You want to see?"

Bonnie followed Miss Wendy to a row of cubbies, observing the other kids as they walked across the classroom. It looked like many of the kids were already friends with each other.

"Here we are, Bonnie," said Miss Wendy, motioning to the cubby that had Bonnie's name on it. "Just for you." Bonnie put her backpack inside as the teacher told everyone to find a seat. "On the first day of school, you'll need a place to put your pencils. So today we're going to make pencil holders."

Woody slid the zipper of Bonnie's backpack open a bit more and looked out. He kept an eye on her as Miss Wendy explained more about the art project. Bonnie sat at a table by herself and reached for some art supplies as a boy approached. She greeted him, but he ignored her. Woody gasped when he saw the boy grab the supplies from the table and leave.

The boy tossed an apple core into a nearby trash can and spilled some of the art supplies in along with it. Without realizing what had happened, the boy continued walking to another table, where he plopped down to sit.

It had only taken a few seconds to happen, but Bonnie was already holding back tears. Determined to help, Woody slipped out of the backpack and down from the cubby. Using a lunch box for cover, he made his way toward the trash can and climbed in. He found a discarded box of crayons and was about to toss it toward Bonnie when a few kids ran by. He froze until they passed, and then he flung the crayons in her direction. The crayons came out of the box and scattered all over the floor. Bonnie stood to pick them up.

Woody smiled and dug through the trash for more supplies—he found glue, wooden sticks, pencils, and a plastic spork. While the kids focused on their projects, he climbed out of the trash can. Without anyone noticing, Woody dropped the supplies onto Bonnie's table and hurried back to her cubby.

From the safety of Bonnie's backpack, he watched her finish collecting the dropped crayons and go back to her seat. She sifted through the supplies on her table. Her face lit up when she saw the spork. Woody watched with curiosity as Bonnie got to work.

Moments later, she held up the spork, admiring her creation. It now had feet, long pipe-cleaner arms, a mouth, and two googly eyes. Woody was a bit confused by the strange art project, but he was thrilled to see Bonnie finally looking happy.

Bonnie flipped the spork over and wrote her name on the stick feet, just like she did with all her toys. Woody watched with pride when Miss Wendy approached and said, "Oh, Bonnie. That is so clever."

Bonnie held up what she'd made and spoke in her new friend's voice. "Hello," she said. "I'm Forky. Nice to meet you."

"Well, hello, Forky," said Miss Wendy. "It's nice to meet you, too. I'm Miss Wendy."

Later that day, when it was time to go home,

Bonnie and the other kids burst out of the classroom, laughing and calling to their parents.

Bonnie showed Forky off to her mom and dad. "Look what I made! His name is Forky!"

"Oh, wow!" said Bonnie's dad. "Look at that!"

"That is so cool!" said her mom.

Bonnie's parents had a surprise because she had been so brave at orientation.

"Since school doesn't start for another week, we are going on a road trip!" her dad announced.

"Can I bring Forky?" asked Bonnie.

"Of course you can!" said her mom.

Bonnie cheered. She unzipped her backpack and tucked Forky inside.

"And they said I shouldn't go to school with Bonnie," Woody said to himself. He looked over at Forky. "We've got this kindergarten thing under control, eh?" He smirked. "I can't believe I'm talking to a spork."

Suddenly, one of Forky's googly eyes moved. Woody froze and squinted at the spork, wondering if his own eyes were playing tricks on him. He moved in for a closer look and . . . Forky's lips quivered. Then Forky sat up and gasped.

As soon as she got home, Bonnie ran up to her bedroom and tossed her backpack onto the floor before darting back out.

Once Bonnie was gone, Woody unzipped the backpack and climbed out.

Trixie gasped at the sight of him. "He *did* go to kindergarten!" she exclaimed.

Shocked, all the toys began chattering.

"You tryin' to get Bonnie in trouble?" asked Buttercup.

"No, of course not," said Woody.

"You could have been confiscated," said Dolly.

Rex turned to Hamm. "What does that mean?"

"Taken away," answered Hamm.

"No!" shouted Rex.

"Or worse," said Jessie. "You could've been lost."

"No, no, no, guys, listen," Woody said, trying to explain. "Bonnie had a great day in class, and we're going on a road trip—"

"Vacation!" shouted Buttercup. The rest of the toys cheered.

"Yeah, but then something really weird happened," said Woody. "Bonnie made a friend in class."

"Oh, she's already making friends!" Dolly said proudly.

"No, no," said Woody, shaking his head. "She literally MADE a new friend." The toys watched, confused, as he leaned into the open backpack. "Hey . . . it's okay," he said in a gentle voice. "Come on out. That's it. That's it. Come on, there you go. . . ."

Forky whimpered as he peered out and saw all the toys staring at him.

Woody continued to coax Forky out until he

finally emerged. Woody turned to the group. "Everyone, I want you to meet . . . Forky!"

"Wow!" said Jessie.

"Golly . . . Bob . . . Howdy . . . ," said Slinky.

"Look how long his arms are!" said Rex.

Forky's googly eyes moved from one toy to the next as he wondered what was going on. He turned to Woody and asked, "Trash?"

Woody laughed. "No . . . *toys*. They're all toys," he explained.

"T-t-t-trash?" Forky asked again.

Woody pointed toward a trash can in the corner of Bonnie's bedroom. "No, no, no—*that's* the trash. These are your friends!" He looked at the gang.

The toys greeted Forky, but Forky screamed. Terrified, he fell over.

"Trash!" said Forky.

"Shhh, no, no, it's okay," said Woody, picking up the spork.

Forky kept repeating, "Trash!"

The toys stood staring at Forky, confused.

"Woody, I have a question," said Trixie, breaking the awkward silence. "Um, well, actually, not just one. I have all of them. I have all the questions."

"Uh . . . why does he want to go to the trash?" asked Buttercup.

"Because he was made from trash," explained Woody. "Look, I know this is a little strange, but you gotta trust me on this—Forky is *the* most important toy to Bonnie right now."

"Trash. Trash!" Forky said. He fell flat on his face. Woody helped him get back to his feet.

"Important?" asked Mr. Pricklepants. "He's a *spork*!"

"Yes, yes, I know, but this spork, this *toy,* is crucial to Bonnie getting adjusted to kindergarten," said Woody.

Forky's pipe-cleaner arms slid down his body and rested on his feet. Woody moved them back into place, securing them with a twist.

"Woody, aren't you being a little dramatic about this?" asked Dolly.

Woody faced the group. "I know this is new to everybody, but you should see how much this little guy means to Bonnie." He paused. "Bonnie was really upset, and I swear, once she made Forky, it was a complete transformation."

"Uh, Woody?" asked Jessie.

"Just a second, Jessie," said Woody, then continued. "So we all have to make sure nothing happens to him."

"Something happened to him," said Jessie, pointing toward the trash can.

Woody turned to see Forky laughing and leaping into the trash can with joy.

"Chutes and ladders," Woody said under his breath as he rushed over. The gang watched as Woody hopped in and tried to pull Forky out.

"Oh, trash. Home," said Forky, delighted. "Trash! Trash!"

"No, no, no—you're a toy now!" said Woody, struggling. He smiled up at the gang watching from above. "Well, I guess I'll . . . just babysit him until he's used to the room."

The toys heard Bonnie coming and fell into toy mode as she came into the room. She went to her backpack and dug through it.

"Forky? Where are you, Forky?" she said.

Behind her, Forky appeared to fly out of the trash can and onto her bed.

She turned and smiled. "There you are!" she said. "I thought I'd lost you, silly." She climbed up next to him with her backpack, and as she turned to look through it, Forky dove back into the trash. But as if he were bouncing off a trampoline, he immediately sailed back out and onto her bed again. Every time Bonnie turned her back, Forky jumped into the trash can, but Woody was inside, waiting. And each and every time, he flung Forky back toward Bonnie.

Later that night, when Bonnie was fast asleep, clutching Forky, he wriggled out of her grip. Once again, he dove into the trash.

But Woody was still waiting inside. Woody dutifully climbed out and put Forky into Bonnie's hands.

"Big girl scary," said Forky.

"Like I said before, Bonnie's not scary," whispered Woody. "She loves you, and you need to—" Bonnie stirred. Woody froze, fearing she would wake up, but she just let out a sleepy sigh and pulled Woody close to her, hugging him. Woody settled in beside Forky and smiled. He was happy to sleep in Bonnie's arms again.

When Woody woke the next morning, Bonnie was still asleep. He looked over to check on Forky, but their new friend was gone. Woody sat up in a panic and crawled to the edge of the bed. "Forky!" he said in a loud whisper.

He peered into the trash can, and there was Forky, fast asleep, cuddled up with some bits of trash. Just as Woody was about to fish him out, the bedroom door opened.

"Rise and shine!" sang Bonnie's dad.

Woody fell off the bed in toy mode, knocking the trash can over and spilling its contents, including Forky, onto the floor. Bonnie's dad didn't notice.

"Who wants to go on a road trip?" he asked, full of enthusiasm.

Bonnie sat up. "Me!" she said. "I'm gonna bring Dolly and Buttercup and Forky and—" Bonnie looked down and realized Forky was gone. "Forky? Where are you?"

"He's gotta be here somewhere," said her dad. While their backs were turned, Forky flew onto Bonnie's pillow.

"Forky? Forky!" she exclaimed, grabbing him.

"Come on," said her dad, scooping her up and carrying her out. "Let's eat some breakfast and hit the road."

"Let's go, Forky!" said Bonnie, smiling at him.

The door shut, and Dolly approached Woody. "Whoa," she said. "He's quite a handful, Woody. You need help with him on the road trip?"

"No. I got it, I got it," said Woody. "We'll just be stuck in an RV, he can't get far. I got this."

After breakfast, Bonnie and her parents climbed into the RV and headed out for their family road trip. Bonnie sat in her booster seat at the table inside the RV, coloring, with Woody and Forky beside her.

Forky's eyes lit up as he watched Bonnie crumple one of her drawings and toss it into a small trash can by the RV door. When Bonnie turned to get more paper, Forky bolted toward the can! Woody grabbed him and pulled him down just as Bonnie turned back to begin another drawing. When she went to look for glue, Forky tried to escape to the trash again, but Woody snatched him up before she noticed.

As the day went on, Woody continued to stop Forky each time he tried to get into the trash. When the family made pit stops, Woody's job got even more challenging. Forky tried to jump into the restaurant and gas station trash cans. Woody stayed on constant alert and always managed to tackle, lasso, or grab Forky in the nick of time.

By the end of the day, Woody was exhausted. That night, while Bonnie's dad drove and her mom slept in the passenger seat, Bonnie fell asleep clutching Forky like a teddy bear. Down on the floor, Buzz made his way over to Woody.

"Hey, Buddy," said Buzz.

"Hey, Buzz." Woody sat up and shifted his weight as he tried to stay awake.

"You doing okay?" whispered Buzz.

"I don't know," said Woody. "I know you weren't around when Andy was little, but . . . I don't remember it being this hard."

Buzz offered to take a shift for Woody, but he refused. "No, no," he said. "I need to do this. That little voice inside me would never leave me alone if I gave up."

"Hmmm," Buzz said thoughtfully. "Who do you think it is?"

"Who?" asked Woody.

"That voice inside you. Who do you think it is?"

"Uh. Me," said Woody, confused by his friend's strange question. "You know, my conscience?" Woody looked at Buzz and was surprised by his blank expression. "The part of you that . . . tells you things? What you're really thinking?"

"Fascinating," said Buzz, taking in his friend's words. "So your inner voice . . . advises you." Buzz tapped Woody's pull string and then looked down at his own voice-command button. He pressed it, and the recorded voice said, "There's a secret mission in unchartered space."

Woody gasped and jumped up, trying to quiet

him. He glanced at Bonnie and was happy to see she was still asleep. But when he looked at her arms to check on Forky, he saw that the little guy was gone.

"Oh, no!" said Woody. He and Buzz scanned the RV as Woody called for Forky in a hushed voice. Woody's eyes popped when he spotted Forky climbing toward an open window!

"I am not a toy!" announced Forky. He pulled himself up to the window ledge. "I'm a spork."

"Be quiet!" said Woody, scrambling after him.

"I was made for soup, salad, maybe chili, and then the trash. I'm litter. Freedom!" he cheered— as he jumped out the window!

Woody froze, stunned. "Hamm, how far to our next stop?" he asked.

"Five point three two miles, give or take," answered Hamm.

"I can make that. I'll meet you at the RV park," said Woody, heading toward the window, determined to find Forky and get back before Bonnie's family left the RV park the next morning.

"Woody, hold on a minute—" started Buzz. But the cowboy had already made up his mind.

Determined to retrieve Forky, he jumped out of the moving vehicle and landed on the rear bumper. He tried to balance and ready himself for the jump, but the RV hit a pothole and he went flying. Woody screamed as he hit the pavement. After a moment, he took a breath and shook it off, rising to his feet. He straightened his hat and started walking along the highway, calling out Forky's name in the darkness.

Woody walked for only a few moments before he heard some strange noises. He turned to find Forky struggling in the dirt. Woody sighed. He grabbed Forky's pipe-cleaner hand and pulled him up.

Woody continued to hold Forky's hand as they walked.

"Carry me?" Forky asked.

"No," Woody said firmly.

"Why do I have to be a toy?" Forky whined.

"Because you have Bonnie's name written on the bottom of your sticks," explained Woody.

"Why do I have Bonnie's name written on the bottom of my sticks?" asked Forky.

"Because she . . ." Woody took a deep breath and tried to think of how to get Forky to understand. "Look, she plays with you all the time. Right?"

"Uh, yes."

"And who does she sleep with every night?"

"The big white fluffy thing?" Forky asked.

"No, not her pillow—you."

Forky sighed.

"All right, Forky," said Woody. "You have to understand how lucky you are right now. You're Bonnie's toy. You are going to help her create happy memories that will last the rest of her life."

Forky wasn't paying attention to Woody. He was busy playing with his pipe-cleaner hand.

Woody turned away, frustrated. He rubbed his forehead and tried to remain calm. "Doing this for Bonnie," he said to himself. He took a deep breath and turned to face Forky. "Okay, like it or not, you are a toy. Maybe you don't like being one, but you are one nonetheless. Which means you are going to be there for Andy when he—"

"Who's Andy?" interrupted Forky.

"I mean Bonnie!" shouted Woody. "You have to be there for Bonnie. That is your job."

"What's your job?" asked Forky.

"Well, right now it's to make sure you do yours," said Woody, still sounding very frustrated.

"Carry me?" Forky asked again weakly.

Woody refused, and the two walked in silence for a bit before Forky asked Woody about Andy. Woody sighed. "Andy was my other kid," he answered sadly.

"You had another kid?" asked Forky.

"Yeah. For a long time," said Woody. "It was pretty great." They walked in silence for a few minutes. "I was a favorite toy, actually," he said with a hint of pride. "Running the room was my job. Keeping all the toys in place." Woody continued to talk about his life with Andy and the other toys. He enjoyed sharing his memories.

To Woody's surprise, Forky was listening. And before long, Woody was carrying Forky in his arms.

"Then you watch 'em grow up, become a full person . . . and then they leave," explained Woody. "They go off and do things you'll never see. Don't get me wrong—you still feel good about it, but then somehow you find yourself after all those years, sitting in a closet, just feeling . . ." His voice trailed off as he tried to find a word to describe it.

"Useless?" Forky offered.

"Yeah," said Woody. He frowned, thinking.

"Your purpose fulfilled," added Forky.

"Exactly," Woody said with a nod.

Forky looked up at the cowboy. "Woody, I know what your problem is."

"You do?"

"You're just like me. Trash!"

"What is it with you and trash?" Woody asked.

"It's warm," said Forky with a satisfied smile.

"Ew."

"It's cozy," added Forky.

"I guess . . ."

"And safe. Like somebody's whispering in your ear . . . everything's going to be okay."

"Forky!" exclaimed Woody. He knew how to get him to understand. "That's it! That's how Bonnie feels when she's with YOU."

"She does?" asked Forky.

"YES!" said Woody.

"Wait a sec—" Forky jumped out of Woody's arms and faced him, his googly eyes suddenly focused. "You mean she thinks I'm warm?"

"Yep."

"And cozy?"

"Uh-huh."

"And sometimes kind of squishy?"

"Mmmm, that, too. Yes," Woody agreed.

Forky's entire body trembled as he continued. "Oh, Woody, I get it now. I am Bonnie's trash."

"Yes—wait, what?"

"I *am* Bonnie's trash!" repeated Forky, running in circles.

"No, no, no, not exactly . . . ," said Woody.

"Oh, she must be feeling awful without me," said Forky. "Woody, we've got to get going. She needs me!" He sprinted ahead, shouting, "Hey, Bonnie—I'm coming!"

Woody chased after him. "Whoa, whoa, Forky. Slow down! Forky!"

As Woody tried to catch up, Forky just giggled and picked up speed, running faster and faster toward the sparkling lights of the sleeping town up ahead.

It wasn't long before Forky became tired and Woody carried him again. When they reached the edge of town, the sun had just started to creep into the sky, giving the shops along Main Street a soft glow. Even though it was still too early for most people to be awake, Woody kept an eye out for any movement. He saw a banner over the street advertising the town's Carnival Days, and a Ferris wheel above the treetops in the near distance also caught his eye. Then he saw it—the lit RV park sign. He pointed it out to Forky.

"Forky, look!" he said. "Bonnie's right over there."

Forky gasped and jumped out of Woody's arms. "Hurry," he called as he ran toward the sign.

Woody chuckled and started to chase after Forky. Then a pattern of familiar lights on the sidewalk outside one of the shops caught his eye. He looked up and gasped. Inside the front window of an antiques store was his old friend Bo Peep's lamp!

When Forky realized Woody wasn't behind him, he stopped. "Woody?" he said, turning to see him gaping through the window.

"Bo . . . ?" Woody muttered. He turned to look back at the RV park sign, thinking before approaching the front door.

"Woody?" Forky said again. "Aren't we—aren't we going to Bonnie?"

Woody peered through the glass and into the dark store. "I know, I know, but my friend might be in there."

"But, Woody, Bonnie's right there," said Forky, pointing to the RV park.

"Yeah, we—we'll have you back before she wakes up. Come on," said Woody. He picked up Forky, tucked him under his arm, and climbed through the mail slot in the shop door.

6

Woody searched the enormous antiques store, calling Bo's name. Forky followed.

"Bo?" Forky repeated as they wound through the store. He seemed to enjoy saying her name. "Bo, Bo, Bo, Bo, Bo," he said until he grew tired of it and turned to Woody. "Can we go back to Bonnie now? I don't see your friend."

"Yeah, okay," Woody said with a sigh. "She's not in here. Come on, let's go."

Just as Woody grabbed Forky, the sound of squeaky wheels coming toward them made him pause. The sound grew louder and louder, and Woody pulled Forky behind a nearby shelf of vases. They watched through the glass, waiting to see what was making the sound.

An antique ventriloquist's dummy wearing a red bow tie appeared. He was pushing an old-fashioned baby carriage with squeaky wheels.

"Is that Bo?" asked Forky in a loud whisper.

Woody winced and covered Forky's mouth as the dummy stopped walking. Its head slowly spun around until it stopped, staring straight at them. Forky screamed.

Woody had no choice. He stepped out from behind the glass and forced a smile. "Uh . . . hey, howdy, hey there," he said. "Sorry to bother you, but—" Inside the carriage, a doll wearing curled pigtails and a frilly yellow dress sat up.

"Why, you're not a bother at all," said the doll in a sweet voice. "We were just out for my early-morning stroll—and look, we met you! My name is Gabby Gabby. And this is my very good friend Benson." She gestured to the dummy.

"Oh, uh. Woody," said Woody. "Pleasure to meet you." He tried to hide his reaction to Benson's creepy smile.

"Well, it's nice to meet you, Woody. And you

are . . . ?" Gabby Gabby smiled at Forky, waiting for an introduction.

"This is Forky," said Woody.

"I'm trash," said Forky.

"Our kid made him," explained Woody.

"Kid?" said Gabby Gabby, her eyes widening. "Toys around here don't have kids. Are you two . . . lost?" She raised her eyebrows when she noticed Woody's pull string in the reflection of the glass behind him.

Woody chuckled. "Lost? No, no, but we are looking for a lost toy. She's a figurine? Used to be on that lamp in the window? Name's Bo Peep?"

"Bo Peep?" said Gabby Gabby, perking up again. "Oh. Yes. I know Bo."

"You do?" asked Woody, eager to hear more.

"Hop on in," she said, moving over to make room for them inside her carriage. "We'll take you to her."

Benson picked up Forky and Woody.

"Oh, um, you don't have to do that," said Woody as Benson set them down in the carriage. "Ah, well. Okay . . ."

"Benson, be careful with our new friends," said Gabby Gabby.

"Wow, what service!" said Forky with a big, innocent smile.

As Benson pushed the carriage, Gabby Gabby stared at Woody, which made him uncomfortable.

"Uh, th-thank you for your help," he stuttered. "I haven't seen Bo in years—"

"May I ask, when were you made?" asked Gabby Gabby.

"Me? Oh, I'm not sure. Late fifties?" said Woody, wishing they could go back to talking about Bo.

"Me too!" said Gabby Gabby with a gasp. "Gee, I wonder if we were made in the same factory. Wouldn't that be something? I gotta say, you are in great condition."

Benson leaned over and inspected Woody's pull-string ring.

Sensing him, Woody turned around. "Well . . . I try to stay active," he said, trying to scoot away.

"And look at that, you have a voice box like me. Benson, show him." Benson stopped the carriage.

"Oh, that's really not necessary," said Woody.

Benson slid Gabby Gabby's voice box out of her back compartment, revealing a small record player. Gabby Gabby started the record, and a deep, warped voice came out of the speaker: "I'm Gabby Gabby, and I love you. . . ."

"Wow, you need to fix that," said Forky, wincing at the terrifying sound.

Gabby Gabby opened the voice box and removed the record. "My record works just fine," she explained. "It's the voice box that's broken. Does yours still work?"

Before Woody could answer, Benson pulled his string.

"Hey!" he shouted. Woody's voice box blurted, "There's a snake in my boot!"

"Listen to that," said Gabby Gabby with an admiring smile. "Let's see it. I bet it's the same type."

Woody squirmed in his seat. "N-no, thanks. Mine's sewn inside. Is Bo around here? Because we need—"

Suddenly, the store clocks chimed.

"Oh!" exclaimed Gabby Gabby. "The store is about to open. Don't worry, we'll take you where no one will see us."

"Oh, no," said Woody. "We can't stay."

"You can't leave yet. You have what I need," said

the doll, pointing to Woody's chest as three more dummies emerged ominously from the shadows. "Right . . . inside . . . there."

Chimes on the front door jingled as Margaret, the store owner, entered with her daughter and young granddaughter.

Gabby Gabby lit up when she saw the little girl. "Harmony!" she said, looking at her with admiration.

Woody noticed that Gabby Gabby was distracted and seized the opportunity. He grabbed Forky and jumped out of the carriage. As soon as they hit the ground, Woody broke into a sprint, dragging Forky behind him.

"Stop him, please," Gabby Gabby said, her voice quiet and steady.

Hearing Gabby Gabby's order, Benson and the other dummies chased Woody and Forky up and down the store aisles.

"He's coming, he's coming, I see him, I see him, I see him," said Forky, terrified.

A second later, Woody realized he was holding only Forky's pipe-cleaner arms. He looked back to see the dummies running toward him, carrying the rest of Forky.

"Woody!" Forky screamed.

One of the dummies got close enough to Woody to grab hold of Forky's arms. Woody fell down as the dummy snatched the pipe cleaner from his grasp.

Harmony passed by, and Woody, thinking fast, pulled his string, causing his voice box to say, "I'd like to join your posse, boys, but first I'm gonna sing a little song."

Harmony turned to see Woody in toy mode. The dummies watched from a limp pile nearby as she bent to pick Woody up. She ran toward the front of the store.

"Grandma, look what I found," she said, holding Woody. She asked if she could take the cowboy to the park, and her grandmother said yes.

Harmony carried Woody out of the store as she and her mom left for the park. Woody couldn't believe it—he was leaving without Forky.

7

As birds sang and the sun rose in the sky, Bonnie's parents sat quietly outside the RV with their morning coffee.

Bonnie was still fast asleep in her bed. Rex popped his head up and looked frantically out the back window.

"Any sign of Woody?" whispered Slinky.

"I don't see him!" said Rex a little too loudly.

Mrs. Potato Head said, "Shhh!" The toys peeked out to make sure Bonnie was still sleeping. Bonnie rolled over, pulling her blanket close, and clutched a spoon.

"Maybe we should have gone with a fork," said Jessie, looking over at her.

"The spoon is safer," said Buzz.

Buzz and Jessie dropped into toy mode as Bonnie's eyes fluttered open. She sat up, smiling, and looked at her hand. "Forky?" she said, confused. "Where's Forky?" She dropped the spoon and began to whimper.

Bonnie's dad stepped into the RV. "What's wrong, honey?"

"Are you okay?" asked her mom, following behind him.

"I can't find Forky!" she cried. "He's missing!"

Still frozen in toy mode, Buzz and Jessie exchanged a worried look.

Bonnie followed her parents out, and the toys broke into a desperate chatter.

"Poor Bonnie," said Dolly with a sigh.

The toys listened as Bonnie's mother tried to make her feel better, but the sad girl could not be comforted.

"We have to find him, Mom!" she said. "He needs me."

Buzz leaped up and ran to the window. "Woody was right," he said. "We all should have been safeguarding the utensil."

"Why isn't Woody back yet?" asked Trixie, worry rising in her voice.

"Oh, do you think he's lost?" said Rex nervously.

"Buzz, what do we do?" asked Buttercup.

"What do we do, Buzz?" asked Trixie.

Buzz's eyes darted around as he searched his mind for an answer. He could only stammer in response.

Rex blurted, "What would Woody do?"

Buzz repeated Rex's question to himself. "What would Woody do?" He looked down at his chest, turned away from the toys, and pushed his button. His voice box said, "It's a secret mission in uncharted space. Let's go!" Buzz turned to the toys and announced, "I think . . . I have . . . to go."

The toys panicked. "Where?" said Rex.

"Where you goin'? Why?" asked Slinky.

"Should we all go?" asked Trixie. "Are we going?"

With a raised eyebrow, Buzz turned away and pushed his button again. He listened as his voice box said, "No time to explain! Attack!" Buzz spun toward the toys again and said, "No time to explain!" Then he dove out the open window. The toys gasped and looked at each other, shocked and not sure what to do next.

"Okay, what is it with everyone jumping out the window?" asked Dolly.

Buzz managed to stay hidden as he raced through the RV park's grounds. He sprinted and took cover behind a trash can to scan the area and consider his next move.

"Woody and Forky were last seen on the highway," he said, thinking aloud. "But where is the highway?" Buzz pondered this important question as he searched.

Finally, he pressed his voice-command button, searching for the answer. He listened as it said, "The slingshot maneuver is all we've got! Full speed ahead!"

Buzz saw that he was right at the edge of a carnival. A ride swirled nearby, spinning and dipping through the air. "Thanks, inner voice," he said with a nod. Then he charged toward the ride, slipped under a barricade, and grabbed on. He held tight as the ride spun, lifting him higher and higher.

From the very top, he could see the highway. He grinned triumphantly and yelled, "On my way, Woody!" Then he let go of the ride, ready to take flight. His wings popped out and the momentum flung him like a slingshot into the sky. But when the ride came around again, it smacked him and he began to spin out of control.

Buzz screamed as he hit a huge ice cream cone on top of a vendor's cart and began ricocheting like a ping-pong ball. He hit the side of the bounce house, the roof of the carousel, and then an umbrella, and finally slammed into the door of a portable bathroom. He landed on his feet in a crouched position and looked both ways, trying to figure out which way to go, when—*WHAM!* The bathroom door opened and knocked him over.

A carnival worker stepped out and spotted Buzz. He glanced around and picked him up. "Rad," he said, celebrating his find. Then he carried Buzz over to his game booth, called Star Adventurer, and zip-tied him to the wall of prizes.

"Step right up!" he shouted to the carnival-goers.

"Put your money down. Get yourself a real Buzz Lightyear."

Unable to move, Buzz hung there, wondering what he should do next . . . and feeling sorry that he couldn't reach his button.

A few blocks away at the park, Harmony plopped Woody into a baby swing and pushed him, sending him higher and higher. Her mother soon called her over to apply sunscreen.

As soon as Harmony left, Woody slipped off the swing and landed on the ground. He was sneaking toward the park exit when a bus with GRAND BASIN SUMMER CAMP on its side screeched into the parking lot.

A crowd of energized kids poured out of the bus, and Woody climbed into the sandbox, trying to hide. A cupcake toy popped up and looked behind Woody.

"Did you see 'em?" said the toy. "How many are there?"

Before he could answer, a dancing doll with helicopter-like wings flew in, forcing Woody to duck.

"We got a busload of campers," announced the sky-dancer doll.

Woody backed away and three Combat Carl dolls—an original, a Volcano Attack, and an Ice Attack—climbed over the sandbox wall, chanting, "Hut. Hut. Hut."

The rowdy sea of kids blasted onto the playground, and all the Combat Carl figures dropped into toy mode. "Playtime, baby!" one of them exclaimed.

Woody gasped and ran for cover, hiding beneath the base of a covered slide. He peered out and watched as a nearby kid launched the flying doll into the air, sending it spinning toward the clouds.

A shark in a boat rowed past. "It's a good day to PLAY! Eh? Am I right?" he said, laughing as he scooted himself up the slide.

Just then, Woody saw a small, familiar-looking

sheep scurry under the merry-go-round. He crawled closer to get a better look.

Woody froze when a little girl on the merry-go-round spotted him. She jumped down and grabbed the cowboy, and when she raised him up next to the figurine she was clutching in her other hand, he couldn't believe his eyes—it was Bo Peep!

When the girl set Bo and Woody down to run off to the swings, the friends looked at each other in astonishment.

"Bo?" said Woody, awestruck.

Bo grabbed his hand and yanked him to his feet. "Come on," she said. Stepping on the edge of a nearby Frisbee, she flipped it up and used it for cover, rolling it as she led him to the safety of some nearby shrubs.

Then Bo gave Woody a big hug, accidentally knocking his hat off. "Oh! I can't believe it's you!" she squealed. They were so thrilled to see each other that they began talking at the same time, bombarding each other with questions.

When they both leaned down to pick up Woody's hat, they bonked heads. They chuckled as Bo grabbed it and placed it back on his head, just like old times.

They asked each other which kid on the playground was theirs. At the same time, Bo said, "None," and Woody said, "No one."

"You're a lost toy?" asked Bo.

"Wait—you—*you're* a lost toy?" asked Woody.

Again, they answered together, with Bo saying, "That's great!" and Woody saying, "That's awful."

Woody corrected himself, smiling awkwardly, a little unsure. "I mean, awfully great! That you—are lost . . . out here . . ."

Suddenly, a skunk appeared, and it was heading right toward them! Woody fell to the ground, screaming.

He looked up to see Bo holding the skunk up with her staff, revealing that beneath its black-and-white exterior were spinning wheels like on a remote-controlled toy car.

"I told you not to drive so fast," said Bo. "You almost ran him over."

She dropped the vehicle to the ground and flipped the top open. Her three sheep were at the wheel. When they saw Woody, they raced to him, bleating and tackling him to the ground, licking his face.

"Oh, h-hey, guys!" said Woody. "Whoa! Hold on there, okay! I missed you, too."

"Let's get a look at you," said Bo. "You need any repairs?" She went into her skunkmobile and sifted through some items in the trunk.

"Repairs? No, I'm fine," said Woody.

The sheep trotted over with a safety pin they'd found and presented it to Bo.

"Hey, nice find, girls," she said, taking it and adding it to her collection.

"Where'd you get all this stuff?" asked Woody, looking over her shoulder at the variety of supplies.

"Here and there," said Bo. "You know, some kids play rougher than others, so I try to be prepared."

"How long have you been out on your own?" asked Woody.

"Seven fantastic years!" she said. Woody was shocked. "You would not believe the things I've seen," she added. The sheep trotted over with an old bottle cap. "Uh, no." She handed it back to them.

Bonnie's Toys

Bonnie's toys

are there for one another
no matter what. They
are always ready to work
together when any of
them needs help.

Gabby Gabby

Gabby Gabby has lived in an antiques store for years, dreaming of going home with the store owner's granddaughter. But can a kid love a doll with a broken voice box?

Duke Caboom

Duke Caboom's kid gave him away after he failed to jump his toy stunt cycle as impressively as the one in the TV commercial. Can he summon the courage to attempt the jump once again?

Ducky *and* Bunny

Carnival prizes **Ducky and Bunny** always stick together—
literally! They hang from the wall of a carnival game booth, wishing
they belonged to a kid.

Billy, Goat, *and* Gruff

Billy, Goat, and Gruff have stuck by Bo's side through the years. These porcelain sheep have a few cracks and scratches, but they can always count on Bo to take care of them.

Officer Giggle McDimples

Bo's pint-sized confidante and constant companion is proof that size doesn't matter. **Giggles** is sharp, spirited, and always ready for action!

Bo Beep

Years ago, **Bo Peep** was given away by Andy's sister, Molly. After a brief stay in an antiques shop, the daring and quick-witted Bo travels from playground to playground, living life as a lost toy.

Buzz Lightyear

Buzz is always ready for the next adventure, whether it's rescuing a fellow toy or being there for his good friend Woody.

Forky

Forky is made from a spork and craft supplies. New to the world, he doesn't understand what it means to be a toy.

Woody

Woody looks out for his kid and his friends. He takes Forky under his wing and teaches him the ropes.

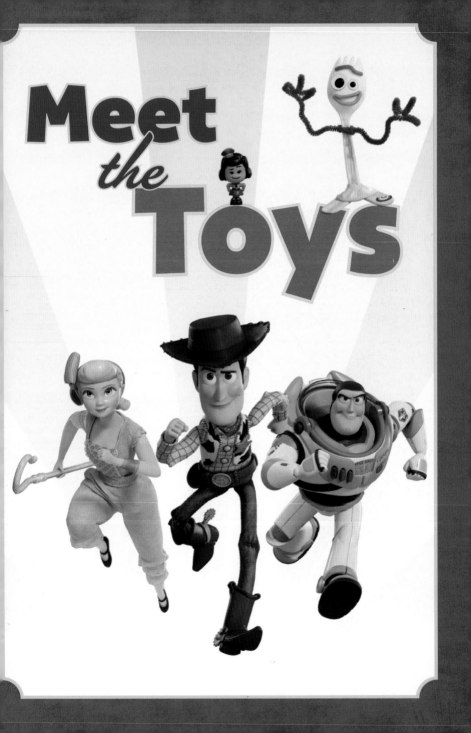

Meet the Toys

Bo shouted, "Gigs!" and tapped on a toy police badge inside the skunk. The badge popped open, revealing a tiny police officer toy studying a chart of missing pets.

"What's the situation?" said the toy. "We heading out of town, or— Whoa!" she said, noticing Woody. "Who's this?"

"Woody, this is Giggle McDimples," said Bo, introducing her friend.

"Hi, Giggle," said Woody.

"Howdy, Sheriff," said Giggle. "OFFICER Giggle McDimples. I run Pet Patrol for Mini-Opolis. Yeah, search and rescue. The kind of pets? Ants, caterpillars, miniature poodles, spiders—"

"HUT! HUT! HUT! HUT! BO! OFFICER GIGS!" the Combat Carls shouted as they emerged from the bushes. Bo greeted them and asked where they were going.

"Combat Carl just heard there's a birthday party at the playground on Main Street," said the original Combat Carl. He asked if Bo and Giggle were joining them.

"You bet!" said Bo. She picked up a roll of tape in preparation. "Woody, you are gonna love this."

"Uh, no, I can't . . . sir," Woody said. He turned to Bo. "I need to get back to my kid."

The Combat Carls looked at Woody in complete shock. Bo turned away to hide her surprise. She couldn't believe that after all these years, Woody still had a kid.

Moments later, the kids in the playground began to load onto the bus. The Combat Carls said goodbye and left.

"So . . . you're with a kid?" asked Bo. "It's not Andy, is it?"

"No, no, no. He went off to college. But he gave us to Bonnie. She's this—"

"You have a little girl?" Bo asked.

"Yeah, it's why I'm out here," explained Woody. "One of her other toys is trapped in this antiques store, and I have to—"

"Second Chance Antiques," Bo interrupted. "We know that store."

Bo and Giggle refused to return to the antiques shop. They had spent years on the shelf collecting dust, and they knew Gabby Gabby all too well.

Bo suggested that Woody cut his losses and head home.

"Kids lose toys every day," said Bo. "Bonnie will get over it." She began packing the skunkmobile.

Woody rushed over to her. "No, no—but . . . but, you see, Bonnie needs him, just like Molly needed you!" he said. Bo flinched at the mention of Molly.

Giggle was surprised to hear about Molly and wanted to know more.

"Oh, it was a long time ago," Bo said, not wanting to discuss it.

"Oh, Bo's kid was something special," said Woody, facing Giggle. He said Molly had been afraid of the dark. "Hearing Molly cry each night broke every toy's heart. And then . . . Bo came into the room." Woody smiled as he remembered. "Her lamp was the only thing that made Molly feel safe. Mom would let her keep Bo on all night."

"Whoa," said Giggle. "Huh. Who knew you were such a softy?"

"And Molly would fall asleep with her hand resting on Bo's feet—"

"Okay, okay. I get it," interrupted Bo.

"Bo," said Woody, "my kid really needs this toy. Will you help me? For old times' sake."

Bo sighed.

"All right, all right," she agreed.

"Thank you!" said Woody, hugging her.

"All right, guess we're doing this," said Giggle, not at all happy with her friend's choice. "Let's ride!"

The sheep were ready to drive, and they bleated as everyone climbed into the skunkmobile.

"Second Chance Antiques," Bo ordered. "And step on it."

A reluctant Giggle jumped onto Bo's shoulder as she pulled the cover down and the skunkmobile took off.

Gabby Gabby sat in her display case, eyeing her reflection in a handheld mirror. She used a thin brush to apply small, perfect dots of light-brown paint to freshen her freckles. Benson and Forky were struggling in the background.

"Benson?" asked Gabby Gabby in her sweet voice. "Are we finished?"

Benson stepped aside to reveal Forky wearing his pipe-cleaner arms again.

"Oh, that feels great," said Forky, relieved.

"Look at that!" said Gabby Gabby with a smile. "Good as new."

"Yeah. Thank you . . . uh . . . Benson," said

Forky, still not entirely comfortable with the dummy. Benson smiled, making Forky shudder and scoot closer to Gabby Gabby. "Uh . . . so, um, when's Woody coming back?"

"Like I said, soon. He won't forget about you," said Gabby Gabby.

"How do you know?" asked Forky.

"You have your child's name written on your sticks. That makes you a very important toy," explained Gabby Gabby.

"That's exactly what Woody said!" said Forky.

"Interesting. . . ." The bells on the front door chimed, interrupting Gabby Gabby's thoughts.

"Hi, Grandma!" said Harmony as she entered the store with her mother. "We're back!"

Gabby Gabby gasped and smiled brightly. "She's back!" She hurried over to the cabinet glass to get a better view.

"Who is she?" asked Forky.

"Harmony," said Gabby Gabby.

"Wait a second—she took Woody!" said Forky. He didn't see Woody with her now. "Did she lose him?"

"No," said Gabby Gabby. "My Harmony is

perfect." Gabby Gabby moved around the case, her gaze following Harmony as the little girl went to sit in her favorite corner of the store. Forky and Gabby Gabby watched Harmony read a short book, then pull out her tea set.

"Forky, it's teatime . . . it's teatime . . . ," said Gabby Gabby with delight.

"Woo-hoo!" cried Forky. "What is teatime?"

Gabby Gabby picked up a small storybook called *Gabby Gabby: A Very Special Day.* She flipped it open to a particular page and propped it against a decorative dinner plate. When Harmony reached for her teacup, Gabby Gabby picked up her own tiny version. She pretended to have teatime with Harmony, matching the little girl's every move.

"Harmony, sweetie!" called her mother, breaking up the game. "I'm leaving!"

"Bye, Mom. I love you!" shouted Harmony. She set down her cup and ran off.

Gabby Gabby sadly put down her own cup. She picked up her book and placed it in her lap. Forky watched as Gabby Gabby flipped through the pages. There were pictures of a happy little girl having a great time with her Gabby Gabby doll—pushing the doll on a swing, dancing in a field of bright yellow sunflowers, hugging her, and pulling her string.

"When my voice box is fixed, I will finally get my chance," said Gabby Gabby, placing her hand next to the picture of the pull string.

Forky put one of his pipe-cleaner hands on hers. He could tell how much Gabby Gabby wanted to be like the doll in her book. She looked at him and smiled. He smiled back.

"Now, about our friend Woody," said Gabby Gabby, closing the book and putting it back in its place. "I want to know everything about him."

Forky hopped onto her lap and began to share what he knew.

"Oh, yeah, Woody—I've known that guy my whole life. Two days," he said. "Hey, did you know that Bonnie was not his first kid? He had this other kid, Andy . . . and you know what? I don't think he's ever gotten over him."

Gabby Gabby nodded, eager to hear more.

Over at the Star Adventurer booth, another kid tried to hit the target and missed. The carnival worker leaned against his counter, bored, and turned up the volume on his headphones. Seeing the worker distracted, Buzz popped out of toy mode and tried to break through the plastic zip tie around his chest.

"*Psst,* hey! Lightyear," said a voice.

"Hey—up here, astro-boy," said another.

Buzz looked up to see a stuffed yellow duck toy hanging above him. A big round blue-and-green stuffed bunny was connected to the duck. They were joined at their paw and wing.

"If you think you can just show up and take our top-prize spot, you're wrong," said Bunny.

"Dead wrong," added Ducky.

"You don't understand," Buzz said as he continued to struggle with the plastic tie. "I'm trying to . . ."

"Cheat the system and get with a kid? Yeah, we know," said Ducky.

"We weren't made in China yesterday," said Bunny.

"No, I need—" Buzz began, still trying to free himself.

"A child to shower you with unconditional love? Join the club, pal," said Bunny.

"Yeah, join the club," echoed Ducky.

"C'mon, help me get outta here," said Buzz.

"I'll help you . . . ," said Ducky, "with *my foot.*" Ducky tried to kick Buzz down, but his big orange foot was nowhere near the space ranger.

"Get 'im!" said Bunny. "Ho, ho, ho—get 'im."

"Bunny, what are you doing? I can't reach him. Help me out here, c'mon," Ducky said.

"Oh. Sorry, Ducky. I'm not a mind reader, you know," said Bunny.

"What's not to understand?" asked Ducky, annoyed. "You're gonna make me say it?"

"What?" said Bunny, clueless.

"With these tiny legs, I cannot reach without your help . . . ," explained Ducky in an irritated tone.

As the two continued to bicker, Bunny began to swing, trying to get Ducky's foot closer to Buzz.

"*This* is what I've been talking about, Bunny— you need to work on paying attention, and your listening skills," said Ducky, scolding him until his foot finally reached Buzz. "HA!" he said, giving Buzz a kick in the head. "How you like *that,* cheater? Huh? *P-SKOW!*" Swinging, he kicked him again. "Ha, ha! To infinity and . . . MY FOOT!" He kicked him once more and cheered, "BOOM!"

Ducky and Bunny laughed and laughed while Buzz ignored them and continued to focus on trying to break free.

"In a galaxy far, far away . . . you got kicked in the head. BOOM!" said Ducky, still laughing.

"How do I get out of here?" Buzz asked himself.

"How you like that!" said Ducky.

Now able to reach his button, Buzz gave it a push, searching for an answer. "This planet is toxic," said his voice box. "Closing helmet to conserve oxygen."

Ducky laughed. "In the vacuum of space, they cannot hear you SCREEEAM!" Ducky screeched as Buzz's helmet closed on his foot. Then Buzz grabbed Ducky's leg and used it to pull himself up and out of the plastic zip tie.

"Whoa, whoa!" said Bunny, wondering what to do to help Ducky.

"Let go of me! Get off of me!" cried Ducky.

As Buzz climbed free, the three toys swung right off the board, landing on the ground in a heap. Buzz jumped up and darted through a small compartment in the wall of the booth, leaving Ducky and Bunny behind.

"Hey, where you going?" called Ducky. "You better get over here, spaceman!"

"Put us back up there!" shouted Bunny.

Ducky ran after Buzz, dragging Bunny behind him. Ducky crawled into the opening in the wall, but Bunny was too big. Ducky struggled as he tried to pull Bunny through the tight space.

"Bunny, what are you doing? He's getting away. Let's go!" urged Ducky.

"I'm trying!" squealed Bunny. He sucked in his tummy, but he remained wedged tight.

"Come on!" yelled Ducky. He pulled on Bunny with all his might as he watched Buzz race off toward the carnival exit.

The skunkmobile remained hidden as it made its way to the carnival.

"Why do you ride around in a skunk?" asked Woody.

The sheep snickered as they raced into the carnival. People screamed at the sight of the skunk, jumping out of the way and wincing as they tried to avoid it.

Bo and Giggle laughed with delight, enjoying the dramatic reactions to the skunkmobile.

"Oh, I get it. Smart," said Woody, now understanding the idea behind Bo's strange vehicle.

"Corn dogs, corn dogs, CORN DOGS!" yelled

Giggle. But her warning was too late—the skunkmobile crashed into the corn dog stand and rolled under the carousel! The gang spilled out, and Bo and her sheep landed on Woody's chest.

"Why are you so bad at driving?" Bo asked the sheep. "You've got six eyes."

"*BAAAA!*" they answered.

Woody chuckled as Bo rose to her feet. She held out a hand and helped Woody up.

SNAP! Her arm came off in Woody's hand and he screamed.

Bo joined him, yelling in horror . . . until she started laughing.

Giggle cracked up. "Ha! His face!" she said between laughs.

Bo looked at Woody, who seemed concerned and confused. "I'm fine," she said. "Don't worry— happens all the time." She turned and shouted, "Tape!"

Giggle dug through the supplies and grabbed a roll of tape. She tossed it to Bo, who caught it with her broken arm.

"Let's get you to that store!" Bo said to Woody as she and Giggle climbed up the center column of the carousel on a ladder. The girls made it to the top and peeked out, scanning the grounds while Bo finished taping up her arm.

"Okay, spill it," said Giggle. "The cowboy. What's the deal?"

"There's no deal," said Bo.

"Uh-huh," replied the officer. "Don't do this to yourself—cowboy's got a kid."

"Giggle—"

Woody popped up from below, interrupting their conversation.

"Second Chance Antiques. Straight ahead," Bo said. "Easiest way in is . . ."

". . . the roof," finished Giggle.

"Let's go antiquing," said Bo, pointing out the store to Woody.

Then Bo took off running, with her sheep following behind. Back at the skunkmobile, she grabbed a sticky hand toy with a long, stretchy tail.

Woody hopped down next to Bo as she swung the sticky hand above her head, twirling it around like a lasso.

"Hold on!" she said as she threw the sticky hand toward the top of the carousel and zoomed up after it. But Woody didn't hold on and Bo had to drop back down to grab him.

Woody followed Bo as she raced along the rails of the carousel's roof. "Bo, how did you end up here? I thought you were given to a new family."

"You know how it goes," said Bo. "Their little girl grew up and didn't need me anymore, so—" She blew a raspberry.

"Oh, I'm sorry, Bo . . . ," said Woody.

"Eh, who needs a kid's room when you can have all of this," she said. They reached the very top of the carousel and looked out over the carnival below.

Woody watched Bo's face light up as she gazed at the children having a blast, playing and laughing.

"Whatcha lookin' at, Sheriff?" asked Giggle, interrupting Woody's thoughts.

"What?" he asked. "Um . . . nothing. I was looking at . . . the *store*. Right there. I was looking at the antiques store."

Bo smiled and turned to Giggle.

"Giggle. Count us down," said Bo. Then she spun . . . and transformed her dress into a cape and pants!

Giggle counted, "Five, four, three . . ."

Woody frowned. "Count down? For what?" he asked.

"You want to get to the store, don'tcha?" said Bo. Woody didn't have time to answer. Giggle hopped onto her shoulder as she finished the countdown. Bo grabbed Woody's hand and jumped.

"Whoa!" Woody shouted while they flew through the air before landing on the roof of the bounce house. Relieved, he couldn't help smiling when they hit the springy surface. He was even beginning to enjoy the crazy adventure as they continued on toward the antiques store.

11

Still searching for the highway, Buzz peeked out from behind a car that was parked near Second Chance Antiques.

"The highway exit has to be somewhere. . . . Where is it?" Buzz asked himself. He glanced down at his voice-command button and pressed it. "Meteor shower! Look out!" said the recorded voice.

Buzz looked up and saw Woody, Giggle, Bo, and the sheep leaping onto the antiques store awning. "Good work, inner voice," he said. Then he jumped onto one of the building's drainpipes and began scaling it.

Bo led the way up the sloping roof of the

building. "So . . . how 'bout you?" she asked, turning to Woody. "How's your new kid?"

"Bonnie? Oh, she's great. Jessie is loving it—"

"Jessie's still with you?" Bo interrupted.

"Oh, yeah, the whole gang's still together. . . . I mean, well, most of us," Woody said.

Bo smiled. "What about Rex?"

"Yeah, yeah—Rex, Bullseye, Slinky, the Potato Heads . . ."

Bo's eyes suddenly went wide and she gasped when she saw Buzz pulling himself up onto the roof behind Woody. "Buzz!" she shouted.

"Yeah, Buzz, too," said Woody. "I cannot wait to see his face when he hears that I found—"

"Bo Peep!" said Buzz, just as surprised to see her.

"Buzz?" said Woody, turning to see their friend.

"My old moving buddy!" said Bo as she and Buzz hugged. "It's so good to see you!"

Buzz asked what she was doing there. But before she could answer, Ducky and Bunny flew in, slamming into Buzz and pushing him up against a wall at the base of the roof.

"Three years!" screamed Bunny.

"Three. Years," Ducky repeated menacingly.

"That's how long we've been hanging up there waiting for a kid," said Bunny. The two lifted Buzz and leaned in harder, pegging him to the wall.

"Look. I'm sorry about that," said Buzz.

"You've ruined our lives," said Ducky. "Shame on you!" He began to sob.

"Who are these guys?" asked Woody.

"Lightyear promised us a kid!" shouted Ducky.

"You did what?" Woody asked Buzz.

Buzz struggled to get away. "I did not!"

"All right, come on, stop it!" said Woody. "Cut it out, now!"

"C'mon, guys, break it up," said Bo.

Woody held up his boot to show Bonnie's name written on the bottom. "Guys, I have a kid."

Ducky and Bunny whipped their heads around. "You got a kid?" Ducky asked.

"Yeah. Now, let go of Buzz and come with me. I'll take you to Bonnie," said Woody.

"W-we're, we're gettin' a kid?" asked Ducky.

"Yes!" yelped Bunny.

"We're gettin' a kid," Ducky said, laughing. The two jumped around and sang, *"We're getting a kid, we're getting a kid. . . ."*

With Giggle on her shoulder, Bo headed toward an air shaft in the roof. Woody and Buzz followed with Bunny and Ducky behind them, still dancing and celebrating.

"Where's Forky?" asked Buzz.

"Yeah, it's a long story . . . ," said Woody.

12

Over in the RV park, Bonnie was crying about Forky.

"Let's look outside one more time," said her dad. "But then we have to keep driving, okay?"

As the family exited the RV, Jessie and Dolly ducked back out of sight.

"They're about to leave!" Jessie announced to the other toys. The group fell into chaos, talking over each other.

"We have to stop them," said Jessie.

"How?" asked Dolly.

Jessie's mind raced to come up with a solution.

"We could frame Dad for a crime so he goes to jail," offered Buttercup.

"Or go back in time and warn Woody about the future," said Rex.

"That's crazy," said Trixie. "Time is a flat circle."

The toys continued to argue and discuss as Jessie's eyes brightened. She ran to the window and jumped out. Rex screamed, and they all hurried over to see what she was doing. Puzzled, they watched as she crept toward the front of the RV.

Bonnie's mom and dad were breaking the news that it was time to get going when—*POP!*—a loud noise cut through their conversation. Bonnie's dad looked up, perplexed. The RV slumped as its front tire hissed and went flat.

"Are you kidding me?" he said, hurrying to the front of the vehicle.

"How about we check out some of those cute shops back in town?" offered Bonnie's mom, thinking she and Bonnie should give him some time to deal with the flat tire.

The toys watched with wonder as Jessie crawled back in through the RV window.

"What'd you do?" asked Dolly.

"We're not going anywhere!" said Jessie. She smirked and held up a nail. "If you get my point."

Everyone cheered. "Nice work, Jessie!" said Hamm.

"Way to go! That was genius!" added Buttercup and Slinky.

"I'm sure Buzz and Woody are on their way back right now," said Dolly.

The toys settled into the RV, hopeful that their friends would be back at any moment.

The gang on the antiques store roof leaned over the edge of the air shaft and stared into the sprawling shop with awe.

"Forky's in . . . there?" asked Buzz. They watched as customers roamed the aisles, sifting through various items on tables, in cabinets, and on shelves.

"Now, hold on. I have a question," said Bunny. "Who will Bonnie love more—Ducky or me? Say me."

"Say Ducky," countered Ducky.

"Bunny," the large plush bunny demanded.

Bo turned to the group, her eyes narrowed.

"Okay, guys," she said firmly. "Playtime is over. You have to follow my lead. We stay together, and we stay quiet. Are we clear?"

"Absolutely," said Woody. "Lead the way."

Carrying her sheep and Giggle on her shoulders, Bo dropped through the air shaft and onto an electrical cable. The sheep hopped onto the rafters. Bo navigated the shadows, leading the group down to the floor and behind some shelving. Ducky and Bunny tried to squeeze through a small opening at the same time, struggling and bickering until Bo's sheep turned and glared at them.

Ducky gasped and Bunny cried, "Oh, my maker! That sheep has three heads!"

"Oh, no-no-no-no—" repeated Ducky, freaking out.

"All six eyes just looked into my soul," said Bunny.

Bo reminded everyone to stay quiet and hidden. Then she led them through a jungle of electrical cords along the narrow alleyways between the store's towering cabinets. She finally stopped and pointed to a large oval glass cabinet in the center of the store and whispered, "That's most likely where your Forky is being kept."

The crew took in the sight of it. On top of the cabinet, amid various items, two ventriloquist's dummies were seated back to back, on watch with a complete view of the store.

"All right, this isn't so bad," said Woody. "We just can't be seen by the dummies."

Bo explained that the dummies weren't their only problem. She indicated the wide-open area in front of the cabinet where someone could see them if they approached it.

"Where Dragon roams," added Giggle.

Bo pointed to a large cat curled up at the base of the cabinet.

"We can handle a cat," said Buzz.

"No," said Giggle. "Not this one."

Dragon stretched and got up, turning toward the toys and revealing a horrifying sight behind him: the shredded bottom half of a stuffed toy zebra. Everyone gasped and cringed.

"Is that what we look like on the inside?" asked Bunny, his lips quivering.

"There's so much fluff," spluttered Ducky.

"So how do you propose we get up there?" asked Woody.

Bo scanned the top of the cabinet and the surrounding booths, considering their options. "We could go straight across," she said confidently.

"How?" asked Woody.

"That's quite a jump," added Buzz.

"We know the perfect toy to help," said Bo.

They heard the jingling of the store's door opening.

"Oh, Bonnie! Check it out," said a familiar voice. "Look at all this cool stuff."

Woody gasped. "Bonnie?"

The toys looked toward the door to see Bonnie and her mother entering.

"Bonnie!" said Woody. "We gotta get Forky now!" He darted out of hiding.

Bo tried to stop him, but he sprinted toward the cabinet. She turned to Giggle and said, "Stay here."

"Ten-four," said Giggle, hopping down from Bo's shoulder.

Woody's breath quickened as he raced up to the knob on the cabinet door. He tried to open it, but it was locked. He spied Gabby Gabby on a shelf above. Forky was brushing her hair.

"Such pretty hair," he heard the spork say.

Just then, Woody was pulled down into the shadows.

"Hey!" he whispered, and then he saw it was Bo. Above them, one of the dummies turned toward the sound.

"What are you doing?" said Bo. "You need to stick to the plan."

"But it's Bonnie," replied Woody. "She's right"— they heard the bells on the door again as Bonnie and her mom left—"there."

Suddenly, the two dummies hopped down in front of them. Benson scooped up Woody and took off. As the dummy ran, Bo's sheep chomped down on his rear end, causing him to yelp. Bo used her staff to knock over a stack of croquet mallets, tripping Benson and sending Woody flying. The cowboy landed on an antique telephone in the aisle, hitting the phone's bell and drawing the attention of a nearby customer.

The customer turned to see Woody in toy mode, posed as if he were part of the old telephone. Benson hid on the opposite side of the aisle, the sheep still clamped down on the seat of his pants.

After the customer left, Bo looked up to find Benson and her sheep gone!

"My sheep!" she shouted. Livid, she turned to Woody. "What did I say to you? *I* lead. *You* follow."

"Bo, I'm so sorry. Really," Woody said in a rush. "Just tell me how to help."

She stared at Woody for a moment, furious. "You really wanna help?" she asked. "Then stay out of my way. I'm getting my sheep back."

"What about the others?" asked Woody.

"Giggle knows what to do," Bo replied sharply before storming off.

Bo headed deeper into the antiques store while Woody watched her go.

Inside the cabinet, Benson leaned over and whispered to Gabby Gabby.

She gasped. "You're kidding! Really? Woody's back?"

"Woody's back?" Forky said excitedly.

Benson nodded.

"And you're sure it's Bo Peep who's with him?" Gabby Gabby asked.

Benson turned to reveal Bo's sheep still attached to his pants, bleating through clenched teeth.

"Thank you, Benson," she said. "Make sure the others are ready."

Benson nodded and exited, taking the sheep along with him.

Forky ran toward the glass. "Woody's back!" he said, thrilled. "I'm coming, Bonnie!"

Gabby Gabby walked over to Forky. "First we must prepare for his arrival," she said.

Forky wondered what she meant.

"Have you ever played hide-and-seek?" she asked.

"No. But it sounds complicated," said Forky.

"Oh, it's easy," said Gabby Gabby. "I'll teach you, okay?"

"Okay!" said Forky.

A little while later, Margaret was opening Gabby Gabby's cabinet to show a customer an item.

"Here you go," she said. "I believe this piece is from South America."

Giggle eyed the key as Margaret returned it to a pocket in her vest.

"There's our objective," Giggle said. "We have to get that key. It's the only way inside the cabinet."

"You can't be serious," said Buzz. "How are we supposed to do that?"

Ducky and Bunny chuckled. "Leave that to us," said Ducky.

"We know exactly what to do," agreed Bunny.

In another part of the store, Woody followed Bo. She scaled the front of an old pinball machine until she reached its double coin slots.

"What are we doing?" asked Woody.

Bo ordered him to be quiet and pushed the coin-return button several times, punching in a secret code. She shot Woody a glare of warning that let him know she would do the talking.

The coin door opened, revealing a tin windup toy named Tinny. The old toy was a one-man band with an accordion, horns, and drums. Tinny spoke using his many sounds to communicate. He was very excited to see Bo.

"Hi, Tinny!" said Bo. "Nice to see you, too."

They entered the cramped space to find an odd assortment of vintage toys from different eras hanging out, chatting, and having fun. Bo scanned the crowd as she made her way through. When the toys noticed her, they shouted her name, welcoming her back.

"Couldn't take it out there, huh?" said a torn plush zebra toy named Doug.

"Hey, Doug—saw your better half at the front of the store," said Bo.

"Yeah, you mess with the cat, you get the claws, huh?" Doug replied.

Woody tried to maneuver through the crowd. "Excuse me, sorry," he said. He pulled his string. "We got to get this wagon train a-movin'," said his voice box.

"Agreed," Bo said. She approached a toy monster and asked, "Have you seen Duke?"

"He's in the back," replied the toy.

She scanned the crowd, and her eyes finally landed on Duke Caboom, sitting on his stunt cycle and smoothing his mustache with his fingers. He was wearing a white jumpsuit and a cape that featured a red maple leaf emblem.

"Look who jumped forty school buses and landed back into my life," he said, gazing into Bo's eyes.

"Hi, Duke," said Bo.

"Who's the cowboy?" asked Duke, looking up at Woody. His height only reached Woody's waist.

"Duke, meet Woody," said Bo. "Woody, meet—" but Duke interrupted, happy to do the honors.

"Duke Caboom," he said. "Canada's greatest stuntman." He struck a series of poses against his cycle while cheering himself on. "Huh. Oh, yeah! Ha. Huh. Yes!"

"Huh?" Woody asked, confused. He looked at Bo.

"He's posing," she explained. "Duke. Duke, we need to—"

"Hold on," said Duke. "One more." He struck another pose and said, "Oh, yeah!" He held it, freezing in place, letting the sight wash over his audience. When he'd had enough, he settled onto his bike. "What brings you back, Peep?"

"We need your help. Gabby Gabby has his toy," Bo explained, gesturing to Woody, "and my sheep."

"No. Billy, Goat, and Gruff? Those are my girls," said Duke, concerned. "What were you doing getting tangled up with Gabby Gabby? You know better."

"Yeah, some toy thought it would be a good idea to wander into the aisle," said Bo.

"That doesn't make any sense," said Duke.

"It doesn't, does it?" said Bo, giving Woody a look.

"Everybody knows the best route is behind the shelves," said Duke.

"That would have been a better route, wouldn't it?" said Bo.

"Wow, this toy sounds like a complete idiot," said Duke.

"He does," said Bo.

Woody couldn't stand it any longer and let out a frustrated groan. Bo smirked and turned her attention back to the task at hand.

"So here's the plan," she said. "We need to jump over the aisle to Gabby's cabinet. And *you* are the toy to do it."

"No," said Duke.

"Duke—"

The stuntman turned his back to them and started posing again, rejecting Bo with each one.

She continued to plead with him, but whenever she tried to speak, he refused, punctuating each "no" with a different pose.

"Please, Mr. Caboom," blurted Woody, "this is really important. My kid—"

Duke stopped posing and stared at the cowboy. "You have a kid?"

"Ahhhh . . . ha, ha, hey, Duke, show us some more poses—whaddaya say?" said Bo, trying to distract him.

But Duke didn't hear her. He had a faraway look in his eyes. "I had a kid," he said. "Rejean."

"Oh, no," Bo said under her breath, glaring at Woody.

Duke's mustache quivered as he began sharing his painful memory. "Rejean was so excited when he got me after Christmas. It was the happiest Boxing Day of my life. . . ."

Duke explained how Rejean had pulled him from his package next to the Christmas tree. Then he watched a TV commercial in which Duke went up a ramp and jumped through a flaming hoop. "Duke Caboom," said the commercial announcer. "Riding the amazing Caboom stunt cycle. Ca-*BOOOOOOM!*"

"I was ready to finally do what I was made to do," said Duke, seeing the memory play out in his mind. Rejean had revved Duke's bike and sent him up the ramp, eager to see his incredible stunt. Instead, Duke fell to the floor. "But when Rejean realized I couldn't jump as far as the toy in the commercial—It's a commercial! It's not real!—Rejean threw me away! It's not fair. Why, Rejean? *Why!*" Duke sobbed.

"Okay, okay," said Bo. "Calm down, Duke. That was a long time ago. Right now we need the only toy who can crash us onto Gabby's cabinet."

"Crash?" said Woody, confused.

"Crash?" asked Duke.

"Any Duke Caboom toy can land, but you are the only one who can crash the way you do."

"I am?" asked Duke.

"Yes! Forget Rejean. Forget your commercial. Be the Duke you are right now—the one who jumps and crashes."

"Be who I am . . . ," Duke said dreamily.

"Who's the Canuck with all the luck?" said Bo.

"Caboom?" said Duke, starting to feel a bit better.

"Who's the greatest of the Great White North?" said Bo.

"Caboom!" said Duke, his confidence building.

"Who's the most spectacular daredevil Canada has ever seen?" sang Bo.

"Duke Caboom!" he chanted.

"Can you do the jump?" asked Bo.

"Yes, I *Can*-ada!" cheered Duke. Then he went into a series of triumphant poses, feeling unbeatable again.

Bo smiled at Woody. "We've got our ride."

"YEE-HAW!" said Woody's voice box.

Moments later, Giggle approached with Ducky, Bunny, and Buzz. Buzz held up the key to the cabinet, and Bo smiled.

"Good work," she said.

"How'd you get it?" asked Woody.

"It was hard," Bunny answered. The other toys nodded in agreement.

"Very difficult," said Buzz.

"Barely made it out alive," added Ducky.

The four toys exchanged glances. They didn't want to reveal what had *really* happened. While the toys had been arguing about how to get the key, Margaret had approached and they all dropped into toy mode. To their surprise, she had set the key on the shelf right beside them and walked away. It couldn't have been easier.

Now that they had the key to Gabby Gabby's cabinet, they were ready for action. Bo turned to Woody and said, "Okay. Let's do this."

15

Margaret carried a vase as she led a customer to the checkout counter for a purchase. They passed a booth full of toys and objects from the 1950s, where Bo, Woody, and Giggle were hiding. Buzz, Ducky, and Bunny were there, too, holding Duke's cycle launcher.

"Good," whispered Bo. "That sale buys us some time."

Woody stepped forward, ready to go, but Bo stopped him. She pointed out the pair of dummies watching from the top of Gabby Gabby's cabinet.

"Wait for it," she said.

The dummies' heads rotated away like lighthouse beacons.

"All right, let's go!" said Bo. She and Woody raced up to a movie projector sitting on a shelf above the gang and unspooled one end of the film from its reel.

Buzz, Ducky, and Bunny wrapped the film around Duke's launcher. When it was secure, Bo and Woody reversed the projector reels, raising the launcher toward them.

Woody and Bo worked well together, hiding in place whenever a customer passed and raising the launcher bit by bit.

"So, how long were you in this store?" asked Woody in a hushed voice.

"I don't know . . . a couple years," said Bo, matching his whisper. "I didn't want to sit on a shelf waiting for my life to happen. So I left."

"You know," said Woody, looking over at Bo, "you've handled this lost-toy life better than I could."

"Aww, Sheriff," said Bo, hopping to the front of the shelf and grabbing the launcher. "You're selling yourself short." She worked to get it across a gap and over to the next cabinet. "I think you'd make a great lost toy."

Woody helped her by giving it a little push, but he slipped in the process. He stopped himself from falling by wedging his body between two shelves. Scrambling up, he followed Bo to a stack of books that led to the top of the cabinet. They used the books as a ramp to get the launcher up even higher.

"You really don't think you'll ever be in a kid's room again, huh?" said Woody.

"Nope," said Bo. "And now with the carnival traveling through, it's our chance to hop a ride and leave town."

"You're—you're leaving?" asked Woody, surprised.

"Sure am," said Bo. "You ever thinking about getting out there and seeing the world?"

"Without a kid?" Woody said with a chuckle. "Nah."

Bo reached the top of the cabinet and pulled on the launcher as Woody pushed it from below. "Can't teach this old toy new tricks," he said.

"You'd be surprised," she said with a smile, reaching down and helping Woody up.

With the launcher in place, the friends took a moment to check out the view. The late-afternoon sun streaming through the windows bounced off several hanging crystal chandeliers, making beautiful light patterns everywhere.

"Wow," said Woody. "Will you look at that."

"This is the only part of the store I ever liked," said Bo, enjoying the scene only for a moment before turning to the edge of the cabinet. "That's going to be quite a jump for you and Duke."

"FOR ME?" Woody asked, shocked. His jaw dropped as he looked out, taking in the distance to Gabby Gabby's cabinet.

Bo patted him on the back. "Didn't I tell you? You're going with him."

"I—I am?" stammered Woody.

Moments later, Duke's stunt cycle locked into the launcher with a click.

Woody sat behind Duke on the tiny bike, still unsure about the plan. One end of a spool of yarn was tied around Woody's waist, and the other end was still wound around the spool. Buzz held on to the spool, while Ducky and Bunny stood by the launcher controls.

"It'll be fine," said Bo. "Duke's the best."

Woody looked at her with raised eyebrows and whispered, "Yeah. At crashing!"

Dragon was sprawled on the floor beneath Gabby Gabby's cabinet, napping. Across the aisle, Giggle was hidden on a tall shelf, keeping watch on the dummies. When the dummies turned, Giggle leaped up and grabbed a chain that dangled from a neon sign, causing the sign to flicker.

Bo saw the signal and ordered, "Go!"

Ducky and Bunny activated the launcher, and Woody held on tight. The cycle shot forward. Buzz gripped the spool as the yarn began to unwind.

Duke focused on the makeshift ramp at the end of the shelf and was ready to go, but then something strange happened. In his mind, the ramp faded away and all he could see was the flaming hoop from the old Duke Caboom commercial.

"Rejean . . . ," he whispered, the memory sending a pang of pain through his body. Duke's eyes widened as he was overcome with doubt and fear. "I can't do this!" he screamed. "I'm sorry, Rejean!"

"No, no, no, no, no . . . ," said Woody when the bike swerved and Duke dropped his head. Woody lifted the stuntman's head back up, forcing him to focus. The bike straightened and hit the ramp, and Woody yelled when they were launched into the air. They soared over the aisle—but didn't make it to Gabby Gabby's cabinet. Instead, they began to fall.

Thinking fast, Woody pushed himself off the bike in midair and jumped for the cabinet. He made it to the edge, slipped off, and then managed to grab the knob on the cabinet door. Woody held himself there and watched from above as Duke landed next to Dragon and sped away on his cycle.

Dragon woke and saw Woody clinging to the cabinet. The yarn, still tied around the cowboy's waist, dangled tantalizingly. It was Dragon's favorite kind of toy! The cat leaped up and swiped at Woody as the cowboy yanked on the yarn, trying to send Buzz a signal.

Buzz, Ducky, and Bunny worked together to pull the yarn taut. In a flash, Bo hooked her staff on it and zip-lined down to Woody. She used the key to unlock Gabby Gabby's cabinet door. Bo and Woody slipped inside and searched for their trapped friends.

"Girls? Billy? Goat? Gruff?" Bo called in an urgent whisper.

"Forky? Forky, where are you?" said Woody. He rounded the corner to hear muffled laughter coming from Gabby Gabby's original box. Forky was inside, giggling and holding his hands over his eyes.

Forky smiled when Woody opened the box.

"Woody!" he exclaimed. "How'd you find me?"

"Bo, I found him!" said Woody, pulling him out. But as they turned to go, Bo stopped them.

"Wait. It's an actual fork?" she said in disbelief.

Forky turned and waved at her.

"Bo, Bo, Bo, Bo, Bo—" Forky said excitedly.

Outside the cabinet, Giggle noticed something and gasped. She hopped down to Buzz's shoulder. "Buzz! The dummies are gone!" she said.

Buzz looked across the aisle to the top of Gabby Gabby's cabinet and saw that Giggle was right. "Where'd they go?" he asked. The four toys froze in fear as they looked up to see two other dummies looming over them.

Inside the cabinet, Bo and Woody heard a familiar voice behind them. "Hello, Woody." It was Gabby Gabby. Benson and the other lookout dummy were lifting her onto the shelf. "Hi, Bo," she said.

Bo held up her staff. "Where are my sheep?" she asked.

"Look! Woody found me!" cheered Forky.

On top of the other cabinet, Buzz knocked the two new dummies down and spotted Gabby Gabby with the other dummies closing in on Woody, Forky, and Bo across the aisle. He ran over to help Ducky and Bunny with the yarn.

"I just want to talk," said Gabby Gabby.

"Yeah, with my voice box!" said Woody.

"Pull!" ordered Buzz. With the help of Ducky and Bunny, he yanked on the yarn and Woody and Forky were jerked forward.

Gabby Gabby reached out and grabbed the ring on Woody's pull string before they could escape. Woody and Forky were now suspended over the aisle. Gabby Gabby and the dummies held on to the string, determined to get them back to her cabinet, while Buzz, Ducky, and Bunny tugged on the yarn, trying to pull them to safety. Woody's voice box sounded every time the pull string snapped back. "REACH FOR THE— THERE'S A SN— I'D LIKE TO JOIN YOUR—"

Hearing the voice, Dragon leaped up and swiped at Woody. Woody and Forky were whipped back into Gabby Gabby's cabinet, and the force tore a seam next to his voice box.

Ducky, Bunny, and Buzz were pulled forward by the momentum. Buzz planted his feet at the edge of the cabinet, but Ducky and Bunny flipped off it. Then an antique picture frame toppled down after them, pinning the stuffed toys to the floor. Dragon turned to the sound and stalked toward them.

In Gabby Gabby's cabinet, the dummies were trying to get to Woody's voice box. Bo jumped, using her staff to whack them out of the way, sending the dummies flying. When Benson landed, she saw her sheep still clamped on to his backside.

"Girls!" she cried. "Drop it!" They let go of Benson and hopped into her arms.

Woody shoved one of the dummies out of the way, but Forky was knocked out of his grip and off the side of the cabinet. Woody watched in horror as Forky hit the ground behind Dragon. The cowboy screamed as the cat turned away from Ducky and Bunny and began to creep toward Forky.

"It's too late. We've got to go," said Bo.

Woody was so focused on Forky that he didn't notice as Bo hooked her staff on the yarn to make it taut and started to zip-line across the aisle. Woody dove toward Forky, making the yarn go slack again. Bo screamed as she and her sheep plummeted.

Clutching her sheep, Bo managed to get a grip on the yarn and swing herself toward the cabinet. But she lost hold of the sheep and they fell to the floor, smacking down with a loud *CRACK*!

Woody landed on top of Dragon. Startled, the cat let out a big *MEOW* and tried to buck Woody off.

Woody hung on with all his might as he rode Dragon, his body flopping around every which way.

His boot got caught under the cat's collar and he dangled upside down as Dragon tried to shake him free. All the movement tugged the yarn repeatedly and caused Buzz to lose his footing. He and Giggle slipped off the cabinet shelf, flying off in different directions. Buzz landed on a familiar-looking bag.

"Bonnie's backback?" he said aloud.

Giggle stumbled to her feet, trying to collect herself, and didn't see Dragon approach until it was too late—the cat pounced on her and gulped her down!

Bo called helplessly, "Giggle!"

But Giggle was gone.

16

Inside the cabinet, Gabby Gabby shouted to her dummies, "Don't let Woody leave!" The four dummies hurried to the floor and surrounded the gang as Dragon raced around them.

Bo ordered everyone to grab on to the yarn, which was still tied around Woody. Duke, on his cycle, darted out from under a display case.

"Duke! Get us out of here!" Bo shouted, holding her sheep and gripping the yarn.

Duke revved his engine and took off, teasing Dragon. The cat began to chase him.

Still dangling upside down from Dragon's collar, Woody yelled, "Wait! We don't have Forky!"

"Woody!" shouted Forky, his eyes wide as he chased after Dragon and the rest of the toys. Then Benson snatched Forky up.

With the toys clinging to the yarn, Dragon continued to race after Duke, who was crashing into the shelves. Woody pulled himself onto Dragon's back and held tightly as the dummies approached, reaching for the yarn. But Bo yanked open a drawer with her staff and the dummies were knocked to the floor.

Duke led Dragon to the back of the store and up to a window. When he realized he was on another ramp, he got emotional again and lost control of his cycle. He broke through a window pane and sailed out of the store with the cat, who was towing the rest of the gang, close at his heels.

Outside, Woody clung to the cat while the others still held on to the yarn behind him. Dragon spun like a top, throwing the toys off and sending them into a pile of trash bags. Unable to stop in time, the cat smacked into a dumpster and coughed up Giggle. With one last *MEOW,* Dragon darted back into the store.

Woody sat up, grabbed his hat, and scrambled

to his feet. "Is everyone okay?" he asked, catching his breath.

Giggle let out a disgusted groan, trying to shake a thick layer of cat drool off her body.

Bo comforted her sheep as they bleated, hurt and scared. "Shhh, it's okay," she said.

Duke held his cycle close, cradling it like a baby. "Shhh," he said.

"Forky's still in there," said Woody. "If we hurry, we can get him before they lock him up."

"You want us to go back in there?" asked Ducky, flabbergasted.

"We barely got out alive," said Duke.

Woody started toward the broken window. Buzz tried to stop him. He told him he'd seen Bonnie's backpack and that she would return for it, but Woody wasn't listening.

"No, no," said Woody, unable to think about anything but Forky. "There's no time. We can easily get back inside—"

"Woody, look at us!" shouted Bo. Woody turned to see the ragged, exhausted toys. "Nobody is with you," she said. "It's over, okay?"

Woody picked up Duke's cycle. "No. No, no,

no," he said, refusing to give up. "We're wasting time. We can do this."

"Come on, Pullstring," said Bunny.

"It's not worth it," added Giggle.

"Yeah, yes—listen to her!" shouted Ducky.

"Nobody wants this!" said Bo.

"I do!" said Woody.

"Why?" asked Bo.

"Because!" he said.

"Why?" Bo hooked Woody with her staff and forced him to look her in the eyes. "Why?" she asked again.

He shoved her staff away and exploded. "BECAUSE IT'S ALL I HAVE LEFT TO DO!" he shouted. "I don't have anything else."

"So the rest of us don't count?" asked Bo.

"Th-that's not what I mean. Bonnie needs Forky," said Woody, calmer now.

"No. *You* need *Bonnie.* . . . Open your eyes, Woody. There are plenty of kids out there," said Bo. "It can't be just about the one you're still clinging to."

Woody winced. "It's called loyalty. Something a lost toy wouldn't understand."

Bo was stunned by Woody's words.

"I'm not the one who's lost," she said. Then she turned to Giggle and Duke. "Let's get out of here. We've got a carnival that leaves in the morning."

Bo, Giggle, and Duke started out.

"C'mon, we'll go find our *own* kid," said Bunny.

"*Mmm-hmm.* You're crazy," said Ducky as he and Bunny joined Bo.

"Bo!" cried Woody.

"Bye, Woody," she called. "Good luck with Bonnie." Woody watched them disappear before a look of determination crossed his face and he headed toward the pet door.

"Woody . . . you did all you could," said Buzz. "Time to go home."

"No," said Woody. "I don't leave toys behind, Buzz."

Woody climbed up to the broken window.

"Yeah. But, Woody, you're actually lea—"

"Not now. Not ever," interrupted Woody as he disappeared inside the store.

"Aaaaand he left me behind," Buzz said to

himself, standing there alone. "What now, inner voice?" He pressed his button and his voice box said, "This planet is under alien control. We've got to warn Star Command. Return to base." He sighed. "I'm right," he said, then crept down the alley toward the RV park.

Woody sneaked around the antiques store, desperately searching for Forky.

"Hello, Woody," said Gabby Gabby, stopping him in his tracks. She stepped out of the shadows. "I knew you'd be back." Benson appeared beside her, holding Forky's hand.

"You don't know me," said Woody, grabbing a pencil and holding it like a sword.

Gabby Gabby smiled. "But I do. . . . You were left in the closet feeling useless . . . wondering if you'd ever get played with. . . ."

"I'm not leaving without Forky," Woody said firmly. He held the pencil higher, ready to strike.

"Can we agree on just one thing?" asked Gabby

Gabby. "That being there for a child is the most noble thing a toy can do?"

"Okay . . . ," Woody said cautiously.

"I was defective right out of the box," Gabby Gabby explained. She took a deep breath before continuing. "I can only imagine what it must have been like for you. All that time you spent with Andy—riding a bike with him for the first time, comforting him when he skinned his knee, proudly watching him grow up. And then you got a second chance with Bonnie. You've been there through all their ups and downs. . . . Please. Be honest with me—was it as wonderful as it sounds?"

As he listened to her words, Woody couldn't deny the truth of what Gabby Gabby was saying.

"It was," he said, and lowered the pencil.

"All I want is a chance for one of those moments," said Gabby Gabby. "I'd give anything to be loved the way you have been."

Woody thought about what Gabby Gabby said and made a decision.

"Just leave me Forky," said Woody with a sigh. "Bonnie needs him."

Gabby Gabby agreed, and the dummies slowly surrounded Woody.

17

Inside the RV, Jessie and Dolly watched out the window as Bonnie's dad finished fixing the flat tire.

"Come on, Woody, hurry up," Jessie said impatiently. "Where is he?"

Suddenly, Buzz popped into view, startling them.

"Buzz!" they shouted. They quickly helped him through the open window.

"Where's Woody?" asked Dolly.

"And Forky?" asked Hamm.

"We have a situation," said Buzz. "They need to be extracted from the antiques store."

"How do we do that?" asked Rex.

Before Buzz could respond, the RV door opened and the family entered, causing the toys to drop into toy mode.

"Okay," said Bonnie's dad, eager to hit the road. "Let's make sure we have everything."

Bonnie's toys looked at Buzz with concern.

Buzz whispered confidently, "It's okay." As the family began looking around, he said, "Any minute now, Bonnie will notice her backpack is missing, she'll realize she left it at the antiques store, and we'll head back there."

"Looks like we have everything," said Bonnie's mom. "You good, Bonnie?"

"Yep," answered Bonnie.

"Great," said Bonnie's dad. "Let's get out of here."

Bonnie's mom buckled Bonnie into her car seat as her dad turned the key in the ignition. The RV engine roared to life and began to pull out of its spot.

"All right, genius," whispered Hamm. "Whadda we do now?"

Buzz frantically pushed his voice-command button and listened as it said, "Scanning the perimeter." He pressed it again and it said, "Laser at full power! Shields to maximum!"

"Buzz, what are you doing?" asked Rex.

"I'm thinking," answered Buzz. He hit the command button yet again, causing the recorded voice to say, "This planet is toxic. Prepare for hypersleep!"

"Honey, will you please shut that toy off?" asked Bonnie's dad.

Bonnie's mom found Buzz and picked him up. As she looked him over, trying to figure out how to turn him off, he continued to trigger his voice box, causing it to say various phrases.

"Just toss it in a drawer," called Bonnie's dad.

Buzz sneaked a peek out the window and saw that they were about to exit the RV park. Bonnie's mom placed him into a drawer. Having no other choice, Buzz blurted, "YOUR BACKPACK'S IN THE ANTIQUES STORE! LET'S GO!"

Bonnie gasped and her eyes went wide.

"Oh, no—my backpack!" she cried.

Her dad stepped on the brakes.

"I left my backpack in the antiques store!" she told her parents.

"All right, let's swing by and get it," her dad said with a groan.

As Woody's eyes fluttered open, he heard what sounded like an old sewing-machine pedal. He looked up to see Benson biting down on a thread, cutting it off. Benson nodded, letting Woody know that the job was done.

Feeling a little woozy, Woody slowly sat up and heard Gabby Gabby celebrating.

She reached around to her back and tugged on her pull string. "You are my best friend. Let's play all day!" The recorded voice sounded perfect. Gabby Gabby clapped her hands, bursting with happiness. "Oh, Benson! Did you hear that? Did you hear it? Isn't that lovely?" She gave the string another pull, making the voice box say, "Time for tea."

Gabby Gabby beamed at Woody as she thanked him. "All my dreams are coming true because of you." She threw her arms around him and hugged him tightly. Then she looked at the clock on the wall and exclaimed, "It's time, Benson!" She hopped into her carriage and picked up Forky, giving him a goodbye hug.

Forky wished her luck and rushed to Woody's side. The two waved goodbye as Benson wheeled Gabby Gabby away. Benson turned his head all the way around, like an owl, and looked directly at Forky. Then he attempted a smile, which caused his mouth to open stiffly and his eyebrows to wiggle.

Forky giggled and whispered, "He is terrifying!" as he continued to wave.

Just then, the front door chimed as customers entered. Woody heard Bonnie and her mother greet Margaret! He peeked into the aisle and could see them as Bonnie's mom explained, "We called about the backpack."

"Oh, yes," said Margaret. "I couldn't find it. Feel free to look around."

Woody couldn't believe it! He spotted Bonnie's

backpack at the far end of the aisle and urged Forky to run for it. "Quick! Before she finds it!"

Forky began to follow him, but when he saw Gabby Gabby sitting up on a shelf across from Harmony, who was reading a book, he stopped. He watched as the doll pulled her string, making her voice box say, "You make me so happy. Let's be best friends." Hearing Gabby Gabby's voice, Harmony looked up.

"Oh, this is it!" Forky said excitedly.

Woody didn't realize Forky wasn't with him until he had made it inside Bonnie's backpack. He looked around, confused. When he saw Forky on the other side of the aisle, he climbed back out and ran toward him.

Forky pointed to Gabby Gabby and Harmony. He and Woody watched as Harmony picked up the doll and pulled her string. Her new voice box said, "I'm Gabby Gabby, and I love you."

"I'm gonna cry," whispered Forky, his voice trembling with emotion.

"Oh, what have you got there?" asked Margaret.

"I found this old doll," answered Harmony.

"You can take it home if you want."

Harmony looked at Gabby Gabby for only a moment before saying, "Nah. Too creepy." Then she tossed Gabby Gabby into an old crate!

Woody and Forky were stunned.

"What happened?" asked Forky. "Gabby was supposed to be her toy. . . ."

"There's my backpack!" exclaimed Bonnie.

Woody grabbed Forky and raced toward Bonnie's backpack as fast as he could, leaping in just a moment before she picked it up. She immediately opened it and peered inside.

"Mom!" yelled Bonnie, holding Forky up. "I found him!"

"THERE he is," said Bonnie's mom, sighing with relief.

As they walked toward the exit, Woody looked through a plastic window in the backpack to see Gabby Gabby lying motionless in the old crate.

"I guess you and Forky were meant to be together," Bonnie's mom added.

Bonnie cheerfully tucked Forky inside her backpack.

Forky looked at Woody with concern. "But what about Gabby?" he asked.

Woody could never leave a toy in need behind. He knew what he had to do. He told Forky to get Buzz to bring the RV to the carousel.

Woody slipped out of the backpack just as Bonnie and her mom walked out of the store. Then he headed straight toward Gabby Gabby.

Gabby Gabby, slumped in the crate, said quietly as he approached, "You can have your voice box back. I don't need it anymore."

"Oh, yes you do," Woody said firmly. "Harmony wasn't your only chance, Gabby, but we have to hurry."

Woody climbed into the crate with the doll.

"What are you doing?" asked Gabby Gabby.

"Shh. You hear that?" Woody said. The two listened as the faint sounds of kids laughing and enjoying the carnival outside played like joyful music. Woody continued, "A friend once told me, 'There are plenty of kids out there.' And one of them is named Bonnie. She's waiting for you right now. She just doesn't know it yet." Gabby Gabby finally looked Woody in the eyes.

"What if you're wrong?" asked Gabby Gabby.

"Well," Woody said, standing, "if you sit on a shelf the rest of your life . . . you'll never find out, will ya?"

"He's right," a voice said. Bo came out of the shadows and smiled at Woody. After thinking about everything that had happened between them, Bo realized that the most important thing was their friendship. Woody was always trying to do what he thought was right. She couldn't just leave him without trying to help.

Woody smiled, happily surprised that she had come back. "I learned it from the best," he said.

"Come on, Gabby," said Bo, holding out her hand. "Let's get you to Bonnie."

Moments later, Gabby Gabby, Woody, Bo, and Giggle sat inside the doll's carriage. The rest of their new friends were ready to help as well. Duke was on his stunt cycle on the floor below, and the sheep, Ducky, and Bunny were in the skunkmobile in front of him. When Bo gave the signal, the skunk took off toward the exit, with Duke racing close behind.

Benson pushed the carriage and raced it

forward, zooming right out the door, passing Margaret without her noticing!

In the street, people jumped out of the way as the skunk raced ahead, clearing a path for the carriage behind it. Benson hung from the handle in toy mode, his body flapping around. Giggle laughed, thoroughly enjoying the wild ride as they jumped the curb and flew straight onto the carnival grounds, crashing against the side of the bounce house.

The carnival-goers gasped when they saw the carriage, and a woman approached.

"Oh, poor baby," she said. "You're okay." She pulled back the cover to see Benson sitting there with his mouth open and screamed! Bo, Woody, and the others hid safely in the shadows.

"Too many people to cross," warned Giggle, surveying the scene. "Gonna need an alternate route."

"Can we make it to the carousel in time?" asked Gabby Gabby.

Wordlessly formulating their plan, Woody and Bo looked at each other with a grin and said, "Yes, we *Can*-ada."

They smiled at Duke, who stared back, confused.

"What?" he said. "What is it?" Duke had no idea what Woody and Bo had in store for him.

As night fell, Bonnie was fast asleep inside the RV, clutching Forky while her parents sat up front, driving away from the RV park. Forky had told the other toys about Woody's instructions, so they knew they had to figure out a way to get to the carousel. The sound of the GPS gave Jessie an idea, and the toys immediately put her plan into action. After disconnecting the system, Trixie hid beneath the dash and announced directions, imitating the computerized voice of the GPS.

"Take. A. Right," she said.

"What?" said Bonnie's dad. "A right?"

"Right. Turn. Ahead," said Trixie.

"Huh. Does the GPS sound funny to you?" he asked.

"Honey, it's fine," said Bonnie's mom. "Just drive."

Mrs. Potato Head sat beside Trixie, wearing only one of her ears. Her other ear was on the roof of the RV with Buzz. Buzz focused on the carousel lights as he navigated, telling them which way to go by talking into Mrs. Potato Head's ear.

"Another right!" he said.

"Right!" said Mrs. Potato Head.

"Take. A. Nother. Right," said Trixie in her GPS voice.

"Huh?" said Bonnie's mom.

"Another right?" said Bonnie's dad. "Really?"

Seeing that they weren't turning, Buzz panicked. "Turn right!" he shouted.

Under the dash, Mrs. Potato Head pointed to the right with urgency.

"NOW!" said Trixie. "TURN RIGHT! RIGHT!"

Bonnie's parents gasped as her dad anxiously made the turn, sending the RV across multiple lanes to exit the highway. Buzz clung to the roof with all his might to avoid falling off. . . .

19

Back at the carnival, Duke sat at the center of the Ferris wheel with a string of flags fastened to his cycle. Ducky and Bunny revved him back and forth, winding up the motor.

"Nope," said Duke. "No way. Decline. No dice. Negative—"

"Duke, Duke, you got this," said Bo.

"This is the fastest way to the carousel," explained Woody. "You made the last jump."

"Yeah, but that was four feet. This is forty!" said Duke, his voice cracking.

"Exactly!" said Bo. "Duke Caboom would never repeat a stunt."

"No," said Duke dramatically. "He'd never do that." But after a few more encouraging words from his friend, Duke felt a rush of confidence. "I'M DUKE CABOOM!" he shouted. "Oh, man, I can DO this!"

"Yes, you *Can*-ada!" cheered Woody.

"I can do it with my eyes closed," said Duke.

"Yes, you— What?" said Bo.

"Three, two, one—GO!" shouted Duke. Without another word, he jumped his cycle to the nearest spoke of the Ferris wheel and sped down it as it turned. When the spoke reached the perfect angle for a ramp, Duke hopped his feet onto the seat of the bike!

"What is he doing?" asked Gabby Gabby.

"Oh, no . . . ," said Bo.

"Posing," explained Woody.

He launched the cycle off the Ferris wheel with the string of flags triumphantly waving behind him. The toys watched in awe as he seemed to soar over the carnival in slow motion, standing with his arms out and his eyes closed.

"This is for you, Rejean," he whispered.

Duke managed to sail through the target and crash onto the roof behind it!

"Caboom," he said coolly. The toys cheered as he quickly zipped around one of the booth supports, securing the other end of the string.

Woody looked out to see the RV in the distance, heading toward the carnival. He hurried to the others. "All right," he said. "Our turn."

"You heard the sheriff—let's go," said Bo.

Ducky and Bunny screamed as they hopped onto the string and zip-lined toward Duke. Woody held out an arm to help Gabby Gabby, then he followed.

"YEE-HAW!" he shouted, enjoying the ride.

Inside the RV, Bonnie's parents could see that the GPS was sending them in the wrong direction, and they were getting frustrated. To stop Bonnie's dad from turning around, Buttercup crept beneath the dash and held down the gas pedal!

"Honey, what are you doing?" shouted Bonnie's mom, realizing they were picking up speed. "Slow down!"

"I can't!" shouted Bonnie's dad, pressing his foot against the brake.

On top of the RV, Buzz snapped his helmet into place as they jerked forward. Bonnie's dad continued to hit the brakes, but Buttercup, still hidden from view, forcefully gave the engine gas. Pedestrians stared as the RV made its way onto the carnival grounds, jolting forward and stopping again and again!

Bo and Woody led the toys as they jumped from one game-booth roof to the next, toward the carousel.

"Got a visual on the RV heading southbound," said Giggle.

"This is gonna be close . . . ," said Bo, tossing her staff to her sheep and taking out her coiled sticky hand.

Woody noticed that Gabby Gabby's attention was focused on something else—a little girl stood alone nearby, crying. He looked back at the RV and then again at Gabby Gabby, her gaze fixed on the sad little girl.

"Gabby?" asked Woody.

"I think she's lost," said Gabby Gabby, her voice full of sympathy and concern.

"Here comes your ride!" said Bunny. The RV was about to reach the carousel!

"It's now or never!" urged Ducky.

"Woody. I think I can be there for her," said Gabby Gabby. "This is my chance."

"Are you sure?" asked Woody. Gabby Gabby nodded. Woody turned to Bo and said, "Change of plans."

Seconds later, Woody and Bo stood alongside Gabby Gabby on the ground as they hid behind a game booth near the lost girl.

"I'm so nervous," said Gabby Gabby. "What if she doesn't like me? I don't know if I can do this. . . ."

Woody looked into Gabby Gabby's eyes. "It's just like you said . . . this is the most noble thing a toy can do," he said. Gabby Gabby nodded nervously. "She needs you."

With Bo's help, Gabby Gabby inched her way out toward the girl. "Just edge yourself a bit into the light—not too far . . . ," suggested Bo. "That's it . . . perfect." When it was time, Woody cued Ducky and Bunny, who were peeking out from behind a game booth on the other side of the girl.

The two gently rolled a ball in front of the girl, catching her attention. She followed it as it bumped into Gabby Gabby's foot. The toys watched as the girl lifted Gabby Gabby up and pulled her string, causing the doll to say, "I'm Gabby Gabby. Will you be my friend?"

"Are you lost, too?" the little girl asked through sniffles. "I'll help you." She gave Gabby Gabby a hug and then looked around. Spotting a security guard, she bravely walked over and told her she couldn't find her parents.

"It's okay," said the security guard. "We'll help you find them. I'm sure they're not far."

Woody, Bo, and the others stayed hidden as they made their way to the top of the carousel. From there, they watched the little girl reunite with her parents.

"I couldn't find you, and then I found this doll . . . ," she explained, happily holding Gabby Gabby up. "Her name is Gabby Gabby." The girl hugged her again, and Gabby Gabby looked up at the gang, smiling brightly. With her chin resting on the little girl's shoulder, she closed her eyes, enjoying the incredible feeling of her kid's grateful hug.

Woody and Bo looked at each other for a moment, overwhelmed with emotion.

"Look at Gabby," said Ducky. "She's so happy."

"She really helped that little girl," said Bunny.

"We did that!" Giggle cheered while Duke posed in celebration. "We make a great team, guys."

Standing on the carousel with Bo by his side, Woody felt on top of the world. He had returned Forky to Bonnie and helped Gabby Gabby find her kid. Woody and Bo took a moment to enjoy the view of the lively carnival together. Everywhere they looked, kids were having fun with toys— some were playing with them, some were hugging them, and others were eagerly trying to win a new one. The world was full of kids and toys, and Woody and Bo had both seen their share, but they somehow never grew tired of watching kids and toys share happiness and love.

Just then, the RV came back around, hopping the curb and landing right beside the carousel! Woody smiled—Bonnie's toys had made it, and they once again proved that when toys worked together, they could accomplish anything!